THE DEVIL'S
GAME

Also by Daniel Patterson

One Chance
A PENELOPE CHANCE MYSTERY

DANIEL PATTERSON

THE DEVIL'S
GAME

A FAST-PACED CHRISTIAN FICTION SUSPENSE THRILLER

RAVENWOOD WAY

PUBLISHING

The Devil's Game: A Fast-Paced Christian Fiction Suspense Thriller

Copyright © 2014 Daniel Patterson

Visit the author's website at www.danielpattersonbooks.com

Scripture quotations marked NIV are from the Holy Bible, New International Version. Copyright © 1973, 1978, 1984 by International Bible Society. Used by permission of Zondervan.

Scripture quotations marked NKJV are from the New King James Version of the Bible. Copyright © 1979, 1980, 1982 by Thomas Nelson Inc., publishers. Used by permission.

Cover and internal design by Kenneth Gorden
Front cover photo © Jaroslaw Grudzinsk
Back cover photo © Sebastian Kaulitzki

First print edition — December 2014

ISBN-10: 0990824209
ISBN-13: 978-0-9908242-0-6

10 9 8 7 6 5 4 3 2 1

Dedicated to my Facebook fans.
I couldn't have done it without your help.

ACKNOWLEDGMENTS

Once again, God has blessed me with an amazing group of people to help me complete the book you are holding in your hands. And once again, I have the honor and privilege of thanking those people here.

First and foremost, a very special heart-felt thank you to my Facebook Beta readers, especially Marc Saucier, Christine Decker, Brenda Duguay, Marjorie Roy, Cathie Goncalves Estabrook, Lana-Wayne Willwerth, Lynne Mullens Hailey, Donna Drake Preuit-Kimbrough, Brenda Reeders, Don Olson, Cheryl Rowland, Jennifer Hartline, Vanessa Winters, Valerie Lloyd Wynn, Sharina Kim, Ronell Stickling, Pam Abshire Gonsalves, Valerie Lloyd Wynn, Cindy Heinrich Jimenez, Tracie Rye, Elizabeth Draper Guerrero, Veronica Sternberg, Kim Swanson Pratt, and Kevin Scott, your feedback, suggestions, and comments helped bring this story to life.

To Jennifer Hartline, thank you for your detailed feedback and suggestions for improving the story pacing.

To Tracy Gordon, Terrie A Steevens, Catherine McPhie, Ryan Froos, Cheryl Rowland, Kate Roed, Jr Bray, Craig Hunsicker, and Julia Slade, thank you for your story and character development suggestions.

To Avi Verk, thank you for your suggestions on improving Samuel Stirling's character.

To Candace Pringle, Nancy Rowaan-Newstead, and Pam Abshire Gonsalves, thank you for your suggestions on building suspense in the story.

To Sharina Kim, Janice L. Myers, Anne Evans, and Jodi Bixler Breese, thank you for your in-depth and detailed feedback and suggestions.

To fellow writer and author Shawn Wells, thank you for your help, support, and guidance.

To Crystal McLaren, thank you for your last minute contributions and our Friday morning coffee sessions.

To my developmental editor Linda Hull, thank you for helping to make this second edition the best it could be.

A very special thank you to my good friend and plotting partner Dina. Words cannot express the gratitude I have for your contribution.

To Meeghn and Michael, thank you for being my biggest fans and always being there.

To my friends who have always been there for me (you

know who you are), thank you for helping me celebrate the good times and getting me through the tough times.

To my mom, dad, and sister, thank you for your unconditional love and support. I love you more than words can express.

To my readers, thank you for your continued support, I am truly blessed to have you.

Most importantly, I want to thank God for always being there when I needed Him.

THE DEVIL'S
GAME

PART ONE

And the Lord said to Satan, "Where have you come from?" Satan answered the Lord, "From roaming throughout the earth, going back and forth on it."

— Job 2:2 (NIV)

CHAPTER
ONE

Seven months ago
Harmony, New York

The sound of heavy footsteps on the creaky hardwood floor woke Pastor Charles Griffin from a restless sleep.

Bang!

The bedroom door slammed open, sending splinters of wood everywhere.

Charles threw the blankets off with a flurry and sprang out of bed. The Bible he had been reading, his constant companion, crashed to the floor.

The confrontation was inevitable. If only he time to gain some strength. The seventy-six-year-old pastor of New Hope Church had been stricken with a nasty flu virus. He'd fought it off once, but he was still bedridden and nowhere near full health.

He stood on shaking legs and confronted his

intruder. "You are not... welcome here. In the name of Jesus Christ... I rebuke thee, flee now!"

The words fell on deaf ears, but he wasn't afraid. *If God is for us, who can be against us?*

But the confident rebuke was all he had in him.

Charles fell back onto the bed, with blood pounding in his temples and his face flushed. His body was soaked in perspiration, and his sheets were damp against his skin.

"You're not looking so good, Reverend," a sinister voice said.

The words struck the ailing pastor like a cold wind, instantly evaporating his sweat and chilling him to the bone. He reached down and fumbled for his Bible that had come to rest at his bedside. His hands trembled as he picked up the book and held it to his chest like a shield.

A heartless laugh sounded from the doorway. "Nothing in there is going to help you now."

The words caused more chills.

The cold presence in his room seemed to weaken him by the second, but Charles looked at him with a steady gaze. "Have...you ever thought...that maybe... everything is working out...exactly the way He...wants it to?" If only his voice didn't sound so helpless.

The evil man's elation vanished with a sneer, as if surprised by the pastor's burst of bravery.

The chill in the air intensified, as did Charles' grip on his Bible.

"You've caused me a lot of trouble priest! I think it's

time we said our goodbyes. Unless, of course, you'd like to reconsider my offer!" the uninvited guest continued.

Charles tried to sit up in the bed. He had to take a stand. There was too much at stake to simply lie back and accept his fate. He pushed his fists into the mattress and raised his body up as much as he could. Huffing with exertion, he stood face to face with the malevolent being that suddenly seemed to be standing closer to the bed than before. His breath was foul and cold. Charles cringed as it washed over his skin.

He tried to wet his lips, but his tongue was dry and numb. He looked evil straight in the eye and gathered every last bit of strength from the recesses of his being. "No!" he said.

"Think carefully..." the evil one whispered, a whisper that seemed to carry more strength than the pastor's clear refusal.

Charles searched for a way out. He looked to the window and then to the door. The man had brought someone with him. A hooded figure stood motionless in the doorway.

There was nowhere to run.

No way to call for help.

There was no escape.

"Is that your final answer Reverend?" There was a slight but noticeable emphasis on the word final.

Charles glanced at the brown newspaper clippings on his desk. What more could he have done? Should he have said something to the other pastors? He had gone to the police looking for help, but even he had to admit how outrageous his claims sounded. The man was powerful, manipulative, and well connected.

But he knew who this man was—who he really was! That left but one option.

Only one.

And who knew if it would work...

He could only hope his clue would be found.

He drew courage from the depths of his soul, courage he didn't know he still had left, and managed to speak clearly. His strong voice carried the weight of the warning he was trying to convey. "I know the truth about you. I know who you are. If anything happens to me, others will know it too."

"So what? They will only fail as you've failed, Reverend," he grunted. "You're just a crazy old man. No one believed you. Even being a man of God didn't help you." He followed the pastor's gaze to the old newspaper clippings and shook his head. "The truth will die with you."

"You can not touch me. *'For he is in your hands, but you must spare his life.'*"

The hateful man smiled, and the unnatural coldness in the room heightened. "Quoting from that silly book won't help you."

Without breaking eye contact, the intruder motioned to the man standing behind him in the doorway. The mysterious, dark figure advanced toward the bed.

The man was dressed in dark clothes and wore a black hooded sweatshirt that concealed his true identity, but there was something familiar about him.

As the hooded man approached, there was no mistaking his slow, labored shuffle or that slumped posture.

No!

It can't be…

He had been a friend—a best friend.

Was this how it was going to end?

"Do it!" the evil man demanded. "Do it now!"

"No, not like this…" Charles pleaded. "Don't involve…"

The man in black closed the gap between them in an instant, and knocked the pastor back onto the bed. With his face hidden in the dark recesses of the hood, he wrapped his gloved hands around the pastor's throat and began to squeeze.

Shaken and struggling for air, Pastor Charles Griffin reached for the man's face under the hood. With the last bit of energy he had, he gently caressed the man's face. "God loves you…my son, and I…forgive you…for what you are about to do."

Charles used his last breath to forgive his killer before the hands clamped even tighter around his throat and made speech impossible.

His old friend's eyes were completely black, and there

was no evidence that he was aware of what he was doing. There was no sign that this person's soul was even in his body anymore.

Charles fought against the inevitable. His body's survival instincts took over. He kicked and swung his frail arms, trying to break the hold. He clawed at the hands around his throat. But his struggle was useless.

His vision was filled with dark spots and pinpoints of light. So this was what dying was like. His starved lungs burned, craving air.

His limbs turned leaden.

His vision blurred.

It was time.

He floated up out of his body, and looked back at it lying empty and motionless on the bed. Had he failed his beloved town? Were its people now at the mercy of this evil?

A bright light from above chased the shadows from the room. Turning toward the light, Pastor Charles Griffin was enveloped in a cloak of love.

* * *

THE EVIL MAN WATCHED with pleasure as the man in black squeezed the last bit of life out of the meddlesome pastor.

This was good.

No one would stand in his way now.

He stepped out of the shadows that pulsated around him and placed a hand on the man's shoulder. "That's enough."

The hooded man relaxed his grip and straightened to stand over the lifeless body of his old friend. He had no idea what he had just done.

Pleased, the evil man looked out the window toward the church next door, and to the garden outside.

First he would sow. Then he would reap.

That was his favorite part.

CHAPTER
TWO

Present day

Pastor James Buchman smiled as he stood on the front steps of the New Hope Church and bid his parishioners goodbye. It had been a good service today. The glory went to God, but it was nice to know he was doing his part. It was always nice to get a few compliments now and then.

"Beautiful service, Reverend Buchman," said Mindy Ellison, holding the hand of her lively five-year-old son, Jordon, who looked as if he would rather be any place else.

Her husband, Richard, said, "I hope Jordon wasn't too disruptive."

"No, he was just fine. Hopefully, by this time next year we'll be able to open a Sunday school to keep little ones like Jordon more engaged." James knelt in front of the boy and looked him square in the eyes. "I had a hard time sitting still for that long when I was your age too. Even when listening to the Good Word."

"I like Noah's Ark," Jordon said.

"Me too," James told him. "I'll try to work that into next week's service." He ruffled the boy's hair and stood up.

As the Ellisons walked away, James turned to Samuel Stirling, who had appeared at his side. At eighty-five years old Samuel was New Hope's oldest parishioner. His thinning white hair was combed straight back and his pale skin was spotted with broken capillaries like a road map of everything he had experienced.

"Always good to see you, Samuel," James said, shaking the old man's hand in both of his.

"Always good to live to another Sunday, Reverend," Samuel said with a wink. There was still a lot of life left in him. "I'm going to have a house guest later this week," he beamed.

"That's exciting news. Who is that, may I ask?"

"My sister's boy, Daniel, is coming home from Afghanistan. The good Lord saw him through some tough times over there and he's coming home in one piece. He's going to help me out around the house."

"Well, that is wonderful news indeed. I look forward to meeting him."

Samuel shuffled on and James smiled as more people filed out of the tiny church and went off into the lovely late summer day.

He'd been at this church now in rural upstate New York for just about three months. His sandy blond hair and his naturally tan skin didn't exactly blend in up here in the North Country, but he was fitting in quite well. His parishioners had welcomed him easily enough, treated him as a friend and had no problem looking up to him for guidance when times were tough. This community was everything a young pastor straight out of Bible College could hope for.

Today he had noticed a new face among the familiar and that very person was now stepping up to greet him. He had dark hair that hung loosely down to his shoulders in thick waves and a goatee that was touched by just a little bit of gray on his chin. He was tall, taller than James, but lean while James was trim and athletic. The corners of his green eyes were crinkled with laugh lines.

"Hello, Reverend," he said in a deep resonant voice, stepping up to James. "Thought I might introduce myself."

James accepted the man's outstretched hand. "Well, it's always good to see a new face."

Looking at him now, he couldn't tell how old the man was. Somehow he seemed old and young, an odd mix of youthful vitality and mature wisdom. His handshake was strong and firm. And those eyes, now a bright green, seemed to pierce him, as though they were looking clean through to his soul.

"That was a wonderful sermon today, I just had to tell you." The man kept pumping James' hand as he spoke. Finally James had to pull away, gently, or risk his arm going numb.

"Thank you, Mister..." James prompted.

"Paradis, Simon Paradis. I'm new in town and just had to stop in to see what the local churches had to offer. I really liked the way you spoke to us."

The man's long dark coat was slightly frayed around the collar and the cuffs. It must have been one that Simon had been wearing for years.

Some people liked to hold on to things they loved, even when it was past time to let them go.

It was an interesting thought and James ran it through his mind again. Maybe he'd craft a sermon about that for next week—

"Right, Reverend?" Simon said.

The world came back into focus. James hadn't even realized his concentration had wandered or that he'd lost track of what Simon was saying to him. "I'm sorry, my mind's still on work," he said sheepishly, nodding toward the open church doors. "What were you saying?"

"I was saying that you sure do have a nice group of people here at your church. A charming couple, Sally and Ben, just asked me to dinner tonight."

"Oh, that's the Larsons," James said. "The Larsons are good folks. I'm glad to see they're trying to make you feel welcome. You know there's another church here in town, right? I mean, if you think you might want to try something different from ours to see which you like best."

"You're talking about the one down on Grand Avenue?"

"That's the one. Branson Miller is the minister there. He's a bit more animated in his services than we are here. Some people find that helps them connect with God better."

"Oh, I'm sure I can connect well right here with you," Simon said. "You haven't lived here long, have you?"

James smiled curiously. How did he know that?

"Your hair and tan. A bit out of place, I'm guessing California?"

"Very good. San Diego to be precise."

"San Diego is a lovely city."

"It is. You've been there, I take it?"

Simon smiled. "I've done a bit of traveling…"

James' eyes flicked to one side as he recognized another familiar face.

Simon looked in that direction and both men smiled as a young woman wearing a set of gray overalls walked out.

"Good morning, Reverend," said Amy Sheridan. "Would you have a moment for me?"

"Of course, Amy, of course." James smiled. "I'm sure Mr. Paradis here won't mind, will you?" He turned his attention back to Simon and then to Amy. "We were just getting to know each other. He's new in town."

Amy gave a shy smile to Simon, her cheeks and the bridge of her nose blushing under her dark freckles. Her red hair was tied back into a ponytail today. "Good to meet you, Mr. Paradis. I'm Amy Sheridan."

"Very nice to meet you as well, Miss Sheridan." Simon took her hand and bowed over it.

"You'll have to excuse my outfit," Amy said. "I work at the recycling plant and this is my lunch break."

"Not at all," said Simon. "A person's value is based on what they are inside, not what they wear outside..."

"Well said," Amy said with a smile.

Simon glanced at his watch. "I'm sure you have only limited time, so I will bid you good day, Reverend, Miss Sheridan."

As Simon turned and walked away, James noticed that Amy's mood darkened slightly.

CHAPTER THREE

James and Amy walked through the double doors into the cool shade of the nave and sat in one of the back pews.

He always enjoyed his time with Amy. It went beyond just discussing her problems and what God wanted for her—the usual things people talked to him about in his role as their shepherd. With Amy, he could be more open than with most people. Over the past three months they had shared a lot of things with each other, and they had become close.

He shook his head.

Those thoughts would have to stay private. Amy was a parishioner who had turned to the Word of God for support.

She perched on the edge of the seat and looked as if

she planned to bolt at the slightest noise. She wouldn't meet his eyes. "It's about...it's about Rick," she finally said.

Rick Mason was Amy's ex-boyfriend and an auto mechanic in town. They were both only a couple of years younger than James. Since they began dating a year ago, Rick had been pressuring Amy to move in with him. She had been dead set against it, not wanting to live with Rick until he was ready to make a commitment that went beyond sharing a bedroom. More importantly, she didn't believe in sex before marriage. That led to their break up only six months into the relationship and the rejection had made Rick lash out. He'd started showing his ugly side, feeling betrayed and hurt. The love of a good woman had been ripped away from him when he'd just expected what was natural to him in a relationship.

James had been counseling Amy from the start, urging her to follow her heart and stay true to her commitment to God. He told her to take her lead from God and trust in Him to show her the way. God's guidance would never send anyone down the wrong road, even if emotions pointed that way.

This had given Amy enough courage to refuse Rick's advances. But he wasn't taking that well.

"Okay, what about Rick?" James asked.

She finally turned her eyes to meet his. "His hours are being cut back at the shop. He says he can't afford his apartment anymore—unless I move in with him and we share expenses." Her eyes changed to a deeper shade of blue and glistened as they were on the verge of tears. "I still care about him and I don't want to see him thrown out in the street, and I think that we could be friends in the future, but—"

"Just not right now?" James interrupted gently. "You've had this discussion with him before."

Amy took a deep breath and let it out slowly. "We had this discussion constantly. That is why we broke up. We hung out last week. He was being really nice at first, but now he is staring to scare me."

Scared her? That was the first he'd heard of Rick scaring her. James' natural protective instincts kicked in.

"How so?"

Amy began to wring her hands. "He wants to get back together. He thinks I'm being unreasonable and unnatural. He's started to harass me with emails, texts, and phone calls every waking hour of the day and I'm not sure what I should do about it."

James understood how she felt and he could see it in her face. Tears collected in the corners of her eyes as she tried to hold them back. Many people today were less inclined to follow the word of God regarding abstinence until marriage. He understood what kind of emotional turmoil it could cause, especially if you lost the person you loved because of it. A strong devotion to God had been what helped him with such temptations in his own life.

"He called me this morning, just before I left for work," Amy continued. "He said he didn't know what he was going to do. He scares me when he's angry—accusing me of being selfish and messing up his life. But he sounded so depressed and lonely. That really got to me. He doesn't have anyone else, Reverend."

"Set your heart on God and His ways first and everything will work out the way it's supposed to by God's will. I know it's hard, especially if you can't see the bigger picture of what He has in store for you, but somewhere along the line you'll realize why you had to go through these difficulties and make these sacrifices."

Amy lowered her eyes. "Have you ever been in a situation like this?"

Fair enough question. Why did he feel shy about answering it?

"Well, my experiences consist of a few dates while I was in college. There was one particular girl that I was pretty serious about."

Amy looked at him with interest. "What happened?"

James coughed. Why did it feel uncomfortable to talk to Amy about past relationships? She was just another parishioner. He pushed himself to keep talking. "We had several classes together for a few semesters. We would study together in the library. We went on a lot of walks, saw a few movies, and had a few dinners together..."

Those were times when he felt he could conquer the world.

"What was her name?"

"Her name was Susannah."

A small tug pulled at his heart. It didn't hurt anymore, but he still felt it whenever her name was mentioned.

"Was she pretty?"

"She was very pretty."

"Did you ever...?"

Amy's question pulled him back. He tried to remember that he was Amy's pastor and her guide. "Are you asking if I was tempted?"

Amy stood up quickly. Her cheeks flushed bright red. Her eyes turned away from his and her body followed. "Oh, I need to go." The words tumbled from her lips much too fast. "It's really none of my business. I'm so sorry!"

James stood and called after her, "Wait! Please. It's fine. You came to me asking for guidance. I will tell you yes, I was tempted. Temptation is out there, Amy. We all have to face it. All we can do is ask God to help us find our way."

She stopped and looked at him, her shoulders still turned away and her feet pointing to the door. "So you asked God to help you?"

"Yes. And I asked Susannah to marry me."

Amy turned back to him.

"And she said no," he answered the question in Amy's eyes, "She wasn't ready. I respected her for that, just as Rick should respect you when you say you aren't ready.

Amy, you should absolutely stick with your beliefs. Don't let Rick or any man tempt you into changing your heart."

"I'm really trying not to," she said. "But I'm worried about him."

James fought the urge to lift his hands to her arms.

"I tell you what," he said. "You head on back to work. I'll stop in and speak to Rick today—make sure he's okay. I'll let him know you're not comfortable with what he's asking for and ask him to ease up, okay?"

The relief on Amy's face was obvious. She leaned forward and took his hand. "Thank you, James. I don't know what I'd do without you sometimes."

He couldn't help noticing how she had used his first name, instead of his title.

CHAPTER FOUR

Allen's Automotive was one of three auto repair shops in the little town of Harmony, but the only one open on Sundays. Fred Allen, the owner, did not work on Sundays but left the shop in the capable hands of Rick Mason.

It was Rick's feet that were visible from under a late model Ford when James walked into the repair bay.

"Be with you in a minute," a voice called out from under the car.

"Take your time."

James looked around at the stacks of tires and neat shelves full of car parts that were a complete mystery to him. The sharp scent of motor oil filled the air but the garage was kept meticulously clean at the insistence of its owner.

Rick rolled himself out from under the car on a low mechanic's sled. He was a large, muscular man with longish brown hair. His face was smeared with oil, making his light blue eyes stand out brightly. "Oh, hey. You're the priest from Amy's church, right?" he asked, wiping some of the grease from his hands with a dirty towel. "I'd shake hands, but..." He held his stained hands up apologetically.

"That's alright. And yes, I'm from Amy's church but I'm a pastor, not a priest."

"Okay. So what do I call you?"

"Well, you can call me James."

"Something wrong with your Jetta, James?" Rick said, moving toward the car.

The 1996 VW Jetta James had parked in the driveway had suffered its share of dings and dents, and the yellow paint had oxidized to something that resembled dried egg yolks highlighted with rust, but it ran great.

"No, it's fine. I'm actually wondering if you do handiwork as well as car repair."

"Not really," Rick said. "Cars and motorcycles... anything that moves is my deal. There are several plumbers and carpenters around town. Why would you come to me?"

"Well, I had a talk with Amy today and she seems to think you could use some extra work."

Rick slammed his fist on a metal table, causing several tools to clatter loudly to the floor. "Why that little...!" He turned away and paced around the shop. "She's got no business telling people about my money problems!"

"She's worried about you, Rick. She cares about you but—"

"But nothing! My problems are *my* problems!"

James continued speaking calmly. "But you are making them Amy's problems. And pressuring her to get back together isn't helping. She came to me for guidance."

Rick crossed his arms. "Ain't nobody else's business. What goes on between her and me is nobody's business."

"Amy isn't going to move in with you, Rick. She's not ready to commit to any kind of relationship with you."

"That's not how she acted last night," Rick grinned wickedly.

"And you trying to make her feel guilty is making her uncomfortable." James finished.

"She sure wasn't acting uncomfortable last night," Rick smirked. "Wasn't acting nothing like a choir girl either."

James tried not to react to that vile statement, but Rick noticed something in his expression.

"Oh," Rick said, his grin widening. "Am I making you uncomfortable now, James? Do you want me to tell you more details about how innocent little Amy behaves when we're alone and why I think you're full of—"

"Rick," James interrupted, "I'm just asking you to please be considerate towards Amy's feelings and beliefs. She is afraid to talk to you about them herself."

Rick's grin disappeared and he bent to pick the fallen tools up from the floor. "She's got no reason to be afraid of me," he said in a much calmer voice. "I wouldn't hurt her. I'm just in a tough spot right now, you know?"

"I understand," James said. "But maybe it's time that you give her some space. You're being too possessive and pushy and she feels like she can't breathe."

Rick looked at him, shook his head and said, "Nah. You don't know what you're talking about. Look, times have changed. Everyone doesn't follow the instructions on how to live from an old book anymore."

"A lot of us follow that old book," James said. "Amy is one of us. We find comfort, wisdom and a clear path in that old book. If you truly care about her you will respect that."

"She's not really afraid of me, is she?" Rick asked sincerely.

"Apparently you have been increasingly...persistent with constantly contacting her about moving in. She tells me you don't want to take no for an answer."

"Well, I don't...but I will."

"Thank you," said James as he stepped forward to shake Rick's hand.

Rick backed up, showing off his dirty hands again.

"I don't mind," James said.

Rick smiled and they shook on it.

"Maybe you'll come to services some day," James offered. "Learn a little about the old book yourself."

"Maybe for our wedding, Padre."

"Maybe," James said, showing a smile that he no longer felt.

CHAPTER FIVE

On Grand Avenue, a handful of miles away from James' church, stood a gray one-story brick building. It was set in place between Petrini's Butcher Shop and TechGuy's Computer Repair. The doors were modern with metal frames and stained glass windows. And over the doors was a sign that read, *Grace Community Church.*

James wasn't sure when he moved to the tiny town of Harmony if there would be enough people to fill two churches each weekend. As it turned out, between the population of Harmony and the five surrounding townships, there were more than enough for both. In fact some days there was need for a third house of worship in town, as his little New Hope Church was filled to standing room only.

It was the same way here at Grace Community

Church, for Reverend Branson Miller. Branson had headed this church for just over twenty years since he returned from his service as a chaplain in the Gulf War.

He had been a close friend of James' father who was an Air Force pilot, shot down and presumed dead all these years.

As a promise to his friend, Branson remained in touch with the family, visiting and providing spiritual guidance for James and his sister Julia. James credited Branson with inspiring him to become a pastor. When Branson told him of an opening at a church in his town shortly after James graduated, it seemed like a perfect opportunity.

It was almost three o'clock now but Branson would certainly still be at the church tidying up after the weekly potluck Sunday lunch. It was just one of the ways Branson and his wife Cecilia gave back to the people who supported his ministry.

Inside the church most of the lights were off and James was worried he might have missed Branson. Then he heard someone whistling toward the back of the building where the kitchen was. There was no mistaking the off-key warbling.

"Branson, you have a minute?" James called out.

The whistling stopped mid-note and a large, dark-skinned man stepped out into the carpeted hallway. The fifty-four-year-old pastor was big in every way. His broad shoulders and firm middle were amply supported by pillar legs and feet that were planted firmly on the ground. At six-foot-four-inches Branson took his place in the world without excuses. He was wise and at peace with himself, the disposition of a minister his parishioners could look up to. At the same time he displayed the caring affection of a friend to whom each and every one of them could turn for help and advice. His benign smile and cordial shake of the hand, with which he met everyone, inspired confidence and urged people to open up and place their trust in him, with confidence that it would never be broken.

"Well, bless my soul," Branson greeted his friend. "James, my son! What a surprise, what a surprise! Cecilia was wondering if you'd stop by today, but she's out now with some of her friends. What a lunch we had. June Foster brought pot roast and the Ladies Guild made a Jell-O mold. You know the kind I mean, with the grapes and cherries? 'Course you do. Mmm, mmm. Good eats. Cecilia made some of that spaghetti of hers with the spicy sauce. We saved you a plate..."

Branson stopped talking about food as he noticed the look on James' face. "What's wrong, son?"

James put on his best smile. "Nothing at all. I just thought I'd stop by."

The big man nodded slowly. "Now you know you can't lie to me or the Lord. Something is bothering you. Come on in the kitchen and I'll get us some lemonade."

James and Branson walked to one of the long folding

tables set up in the dining area. The kitchen was on the other side of a low wall. Branson's congregation had worked hard to clean the place up after their meal. The pots all hung from their own hooks. The dishes were put away. The floor had been swept and a small pile of dirt stood in the corner with a broom leaning over it, guarding it, until it could be swept into a dustpan and thrown out. All said, the place was clean and tidy with everything in its place. No small feat, considering that probably close to seventy people had just shared a meal there.

Branson put two tall glasses of pale yellow lemonade on the table as he sat down across from James. His large hands covered James' own. With eyes closed, he spoke a simple prayer. "Lord, Father, please lift whatever burden is on my friend's shoulders today. Let us be able to help each other and continue to be Your instruments. Thank you, Lord. Amen."

"Amen," James responded.

They both sipped their lemonade before Branson eyed James and leaned back in his folding chair. "So what's got you so down today?"

James cleared his throat. The lemonade was fantastic. Sweet and tart at the same time. He took another drink and then motioned helplessly with one hand. "I guess I'm feeling the weight of some of my parishioners' problems."

"Oh!"

"I feel like there is more I could be doing."

"You aren't supposed to take them on son. You know

that."

"But I—"

"But nothing. Your job is to show them that God will take on their problems," Branson said, as he opened a worn leather-bound Bible on the table and read from Psalm 55:22. "'*Cast your cares on the Lord and he will sustain you; he will never let the righteous be shaken.*'"

James smiled at his mentor. He knew the Bible like most people knew the lyrics to their favorite song. It was nice to have him this close that he could stop in at any time to talk.

"I know that, but I'm a fixer."

Branson waved his hands. "Son, learn to rejoice in your problems. God will use them to your benefit." He turned to Romans 5:3-4. "'*Because we know that suffering produces perseverance; perseverance, character; and character, hope.*'"

James rubbed his chin. "But my flock expects me to have answers. And I want to give them those answers."

"You already have the answer, son."

The answer was God but James still wanted to take part and solve the world's ills. Would that be his downfall? "You know me well enough to understand that's the most difficult part of my job. I want to help. I want action. It's in my blood."

Since becoming the man of the family, James had always been the one to solve the problems.

"I understand," Branson nodded. "Your father was the

29

same way, always wanting to rush in and save the world. But that is up to God. You just need to trust."

"I know this. I do—"

"But not when you feel there has been a call to action?" Branson finished.

"Right."

Branson leaned forward and put a large hand on James' arm. "There is only one solution son. God. He will solve anyone's problems. The person just has to ask."

James sighed. He'd been called to be a minister, but sometimes it was like God was playing a joke on him—or teaching him a lesson. He was never sure which. Branson was right. He had to step back and let God be the answer. Let God be the problem solver. "There is something else..."

"Something serious?"

"I think so. One of my parishioners is having issues with her ex-boyfriend. She came to talk to me today after my service."

"Uh, huh,"

"This isn't the first time she's come to me about him. She's a really nice girl. I hate to see her upset this way."

"Uh, huh," Branson said again, seeing right through James. "And..."

"And I don't know if I am being completely objective with advising her of the Lord's path for purely her own sake...or mine."

"Does it make a difference?" Branson asked, taking another sip of lemonade.

James was surprised. "Well, of course it does!"

"Why?" asked Branson. "You are telling her to follow God's Word, aren't you?"

"Yes, but I think I may be doing it for selfish reasons."

"That's nonsense. It's your job as a pastor and your duty as a man of God. There can be no selfish motives in that. You spread the word of God, son. You show them the way. It's up to them to follow it or not. Now that's all the reverend-to-reverend advice I'm going to give you on that. What I'm going to say next is man-to-man. Getting hung up on a girl who is having difficulties with another man will only put both of you into a tight spot."

"I went to talk to the ex-boyfriend today," James said.

Branson looked at him with an arched eyebrow.

"She asked me to…"

Branson kept his eyebrow up.

"I told her I would."

"And how did that work out?"

"Not bad," James said. "He didn't punch me or throw anything directly at me. I just asked him to respect her wishes and her beliefs. He said that he would."

"Do you believe him?"

"I'd like to."

"But you'd also like him out of the picture altogether. Maybe far away from here in another mechanic shop in another town?"

James looked at his friend and mentor with widened eyes, wondering how he could know that Rick worked in an auto shop.

"You smell like motor oil, son. And your hands are stained." Branson grinned at him. "Detective work was my second calling. Never followed it."

"Maybe you should have," James said.

"It's nice to know I have something to fall back on should this whole preacher-thing not work out," Branson said with a smile. "Now, listen to me, son. It sounds like this young woman already has her hands full sorting out her feelings for one young man. You do not need to add anything else to the mix."

"You are right," James sighed. "I should know better."

Branson stood, collected the empty lemonade glasses and took them to the sink. He opened the refrigerator and took out a plastic container. "She is just having a tough time, and she's lucky that she has you as a supportive advisor and friend."

"A supportive advisor and friend," James said, wishing he relished that role more than he did. "I'll pray to do my best at just that."

Branson sat down across from him. "You're a good, kind man, James. The good Lord will bless you with the right woman when He sees fit, just like He blessed me with Cecilia."

Branson slid the container in front of James. "Here's your spaghetti."

"Thank you for the advice and the meal."

"Anytime, son. Anytime."

CHAPTER
SIX

———

On Wednesday afternoon, James led the New Hope Church Community Outreach Partners in a prayer before going over their weekly plan. Several members of their congregation were homebound or needed extra help in one form or another. The COPs, as they called themselves, made sure those people had everything they needed, from trips to the doctor, groceries and hot meals to a friend to talk to.

Amy took Wednesdays off and was always an enthusiastic participant. Dressed in blue jeans and a flowered t-shirt she took the lead after James' prayer, walking to the front of the church with her clipboard in hand.

"Thank you, Reverend Buchman. Hello, fellow COPs.

First of all, I want us to welcome our newest member, Simon Paradis. He's new in town and I think it's great that he wants to start helping our community."

All heads turned toward Simon who stood up from his second pew seat and nodded graciously at everyone's greeting.

"We have a few changes from last week. Let's remember that Mrs. Thomas is lactose intolerant, so no more cheese on her sandwiches please. We have a new person in need for a few weeks. Debra Carter broke her ankle and she'll need a little help getting her kids off to school in the mornings and back home again. A couple of our regulars, Emily Watson and George Alvarez, have come down with some flu symptoms. We need to keep a special eye on them because that can be very dangerous for the elderly. I'd like to go over our usual assignments now..."

James watched from the front pew and admired how Amy was able to take charge and organize the group. She seemed much happier today than she had on Sunday and he was truly glad for her.

When the briefing was over there was time for refreshments before everyone went on their rounds. A couple of folding tables were set up with coffee, cookies and brownies.

"These brownies are absolutely sinful!" exclaimed Simon, munching away.

Georgette Newman, the baker, stood next to him

beaming.

"Reverend, are you sure these should be allowed in a church?" Simon asked in a joking tone.

James smiled, "Well, they were made by a good woman with nothing but pure ingredients and pure intent," he said. "I see nothing sinful about that." He picked up a brownie and took a bite. It was truly delicious. "In moderation, of course. These could lead to serious gluttony very easily," he cautioned with exaggerated seriousness.

"That's why I make only small batches," Georgette sighed.

They all shared a laugh.

Simon picked up another brownie and slipped it into the pocket of his overcoat. "I'll just take one more of these for the ride."

"Mr. Paradis, would you like to ride with me on my delivery route?" Georgette asked.

"Nothing would please me more, my good woman."

Georgette gave him instructions as to how to pack up and he dutifully followed her lead.

James looked over the heads of the thinning crowd. People were carrying boxes to their cars and tidying up. He picked up a care box himself and stepped outside, searching for Amy. He spotted her loading a care box into the trunk of Rick's car. Rick spotted him first and gave him a wave and a smile. James waved back. It looked as if his talk with Rick did some good. They seemed to be getting along quite nicely. Amy turned around and flashed a big smile as she got into the front passenger seat and waved goodbye.

Alone on the steps of his church, James gave silent thanks to God for the wonderful turnout of helpful people in his parish and walked to his car.

CHAPTER SEVEN

James' delivery was for Samuel Stirling. He drove down Barrington Drive to Samuel's house just fifteen minutes away from the church.

Samuel was a World War II veteran and still worked a couple days a week as a janitor at a local warehouse. He had never married and had no children to look after him. He had been partially blind in one eye since 1945, but still had his driver's license. Now, his other eye was starting to fail him. After a long independent life, he was facing the reality that he might end up in a nursing home. But what Samuel missed most was just having someone to talk to.

Samuel lived in a small double-wide home that had seen better days. The blue paint was peeling in places and the roofing tiles needed to be replaced. But the lawn was tidy, and James knew from having been inside that the interior was a bright and cheerful place with pictures of friends and family, most now departed, hanging proudly on display. Samuel wasn't at all bitter about where his life had led him. God had been good to him, Samuel had told James many times, and when it was his time to go he looked forward to the opportunity to thank God in person.

When James walked up to the front door with his care package, the door opened before he reached it. A large, muscular young man with crew-cut blond hair stepped out and approached him.

"Sir," he said. "Let me take that for you..."

James let him have the box. It didn't seem negotiable.

"Hello!" called Samuel. "Welcome, Reverend!"

"Hello," James said, following the young man into Samuel's home.

James' eyes took in the colorful decor of the interior and had to smile at the festive atmosphere. The furniture was pristine 1960s Danish Modern, upholstered in the olive and orange colors popular in that time. Red and gold floral drapes were pulled back revealing lace curtains that let in the bright sunlight and made the place really sparkle. Samuel stood up from his favorite lounger, and beckoned James in. "Please, let me introduce you to my nephew, Daniel Lapinski."

The young man who had taken the package now set it on the dining table and then turned around with a smile and an extended hand, looking much less intimidating than before. "Pleased to meet you, Reverend."

James took the man's hand and tried not to wince at the powerful grip. "Nice to meet you too, Daniel. Your uncle told me you were coming back from Afghanistan soon. Welcome home. I appreciate what you are doing for us over there."

"Thank you, sir. It's good to be back."

"You don't have to call me sir," James told him.

"Sorry, sir. It's a habit. Would you like some coffee? I made a fresh pot. Uncle Samuel told me you'd be coming."

"Sure," said James. One of the duties of the COPs delivery program was to socialize, so he had planned on spending some time. "I've got some of Georgette Newman's brownies in the care box. They'll go wonderfully with some coffee." He stepped toward the box to get the brownies, but Daniel got there first.

"Please sit down, sir," Daniel told him. "You are our guest." He took the bag of brownies out and began to arrange them on one of Samuel's china plates along with a coffee pot and matching cups with saucers. James grinned watching the man's big hands carefully handling the delicate set.

Samuel said, as James took a seat on the couch, "It turns out that Daniel is a wonderful house guest. He won't let me do a thing. Even cooks and cleans for me."

"It's the least I can do," Daniel said. He brought the tray into the living room and placed it on the coffee table. "Uncle Samuel is going to let me stay with him for a couple of months while I figure out what I'm going to do now that I'm back home for good."

"He's going to patch up my roof, put on a coat of paint..."

"And I think a little front porch would be a nice addition, don't you, sir?" Daniel asked. He gave his uncle a cup of coffee, already prepared with cream and sugar.

"I think that would be splendid," beamed Samuel, biting into a brownie.

"Me too," said James. He helped himself to a cup. "You do carpentry work, Daniel?"

"Yes sir and yard work, landscaping. Do you know of anyone who needs work after I get finished around here? I could really use the money."

James smiled. "As a matter of fact, I do. I'll start spreading the word."

CHAPTER EIGHT

The rest of that Wednesday afternoon passed as quickly and smoothly as a warm summer breeze. James sat at his desk in the back room of the church and poured over financial statements. As he tried to make the books balance, there was a knock at the door.

"Come in," he called out, setting down his pen on top of a growing pile of paperwork.

The door opened on creaky hinges and the smiling face of Simon Paradis appeared.

"Excuse me, Reverend," he said, stepping into the room. "I wanted to thank you for letting me help out with COPs today."

"Thank you, Simon. We appreciate the help."

He noticed that Simon still wore his long dark coat with the frayed cuffs, even though it was a very warm day.

Some people liked to hold on to things they loved, even when it was past time for them to let them go.

Maybe he should craft a sermon about that for next week—

"Right, Reverend?"

James blinked, almost forgetting Simon was standing right in front of him. "I'm sorry, I must have zoned out." He had the strangest feeling of déjà vu. "You were saying?"

"I was saying that the people here have been so inviting. I am so glad to have moved to this town and joined your church."

"Well, you've managed to integrate very well," James said. "Helping out with community events is a wonderful way to make friends."

"It's always been my policy to seek out new friends wherever I go," said Simon with a pious smile that seemed a little too pious.

James looked at him curiously. Right from the start everyone in town seemed to be falling over themselves to make Simon feel welcome. He had never seen anyone make themselves a part of the community so quickly— even when he came and took over the New Hope Church.

"I'll be having dinner again with that nice couple, Sally and Ben, tomorrow night."

"I'm glad to see they're making you feel welcome," James nodded, trying to dismiss his slight feelings of envy.

"Reverend Buchman?" a young woman's voice called out.

"Amy, please come on in."

Simon turned his wide smile on Amy, as she entered the office. "Miss Sheridan, wonderful to see you again."

"Oh, Mr. Paradis! I want to thank you for helping out this afternoon. Am I interrupting?"

"No, not at all," James said quickly.

"He's right," said Simon. "I was just thanking the Reverend for the opportunity to help out my new community."

"Well, accept my thanks too," Amy said.

Simon gave a slight bow. "Entirely my pleasure, I assure you. And now, I'll be going. I'll see you again. I'm sure of it."

"Amy," James said, turning his attention to her and gesturing to the chair on the other side of his desk. "Please sit with me."

Amy seemed happy and confident. She was practically glowing.

"I want to thank you for talking to Rick the other day. He has been much more respectful."

"I'm glad to hear it," James said.

"You saw today that he even wanted to help out with the COPs. I made a volunteer out of him!"

"Yes, I noticed that. Good job. He still isn't ready to attend service, though?"

Amy grinned. "No, but I'm working on it. He says he's ready to be just friends with me."

James nodded supportively.

"He came over last night and made dinner for me... but he didn't spend the night," she added hurriedly. "But I know he wanted to..." She looked at James pleadingly with her big blue eyes.

"Temptation is something we all have to deal with," James said.

"Am I sending him the wrong message? I'm afraid I might fall into some old habits, and I needed to talk to you."

"Amy," James said, placing a hand gently over her right wrist, "some people like to hold on to things, even when it's way past time to let go. Maybe that's what you're doing with your beliefs. It's time to let them go."

He heard the words as they came out of his mouth.

Whoa!

Just, hold on a minute here.

Where had that come from?

How could he possibly be suggesting to Amy that she give up her ideas of right and wrong just to make a man feel better? He would never suggest such a thing.

But, he had.

Amy watched him, her eyes wide, as he tried to nail down the root of that thought.

Then he had it—the thought had come into his mind when Simon had been talking to him. It came so strongly that he had lost track of what was going on around him. Have the uneasy feelings he had every time while talking to Simon been more on point than he realized?

"Reverend?" Amy said with a confused look on her face.

"Um, sorry, Amy, I lost my train of thought there. What I meant to say was to *stick* with your beliefs. Temptation will always be around, but if you set your heart on God and His ways first, the right decision will come to you."

"I've prayed about it, Reverend. And I'm standing firm on this. I told Rick I care about our friendship, but when I take that next step it will be with the man I will spend the rest of my life with—my husband. I want that moment to be special in the lives of my partner and I, and in the eyes of God. Rick says he understands. He still talks about us getting married someday, but I really don't see that kind of a future with him."

"Just follow your heart."

She stood up. "Rick and I will stay just friends. He isn't the right man for me. I know that. God will show me the right man when He's ready."

Was there more to Amy's words than was on the surface?

CHAPTER NINE

___

Late Wednesday evening, James sat alone at his desk. He thought about his mental stumble with Amy as he ate his dinner, consisting of a tomato sandwich and barbecue flavored potato chips. It wasn't like him to be so easily swayed by an invasive thought like that.

It made no sense. That thought had taken root in his mind while talking to Simon and grown into a living thing that came out of his lips at just the wrong time. He was still mortified that he had actually said those words to Amy.

Amy.

Now that was a topic he didn't need to cloud his mind. He shook his head and reminded himself of Branson's warning to keep a respectful distance.

He washed down the last of his sandwich with a bottle of grape soda. His mind was wandering too much, and he didn't really know what he was trying to convince himself of.

Brushing his hands together to clean off the crumbs, James stood and walked out into the main room of the church, closing and locking the office door behind him. The church was a small building and the nave with its rows of wooden pews set up facing the altar seemed crammed together even when they stood empty.

James stopped short.

He wasn't alone.

CHAPTER
TEN

—

"Hello, Reverend," Simon Paradis said with a nod. He sat there, lounging in the front row, one arm hanging over the back of the bench, his long legs crossed at the ankles and sticking straight out. That same smile from earlier was still in place.

"Hello again, Simon," James said, feeling defensive right away. "Did you need something?"

"Well yes, actually Reverend, I do or, more accurately, I did. I needed you to pass that message along to your friend Amy. I'm glad to know that you did."

"I beg your pardon?"

"You countered it pretty quickly and that was a disappointment, but I think she got the drift."

The air was suddenly chilly, almost cold.

"I've got a lot of work to do, Simon..."

"You and I both, Reverend." Simon unfolded himself slowly and stood up from the bench, his body seeming to float up onto his feet. He took a moment to brush the dust from his coat and said, "I like people. I like helping them out. You and I aren't at all different in that respect."

James gazed at the man's smile. It was a perfect smile. It was a happy smile. It was a smile of a man who wanted other people to be happy. It was the smile of a man who wanted James to be happy.

He should do whatever he could to be happy. Just be happy—

James snapped his head back up. He had been falling asleep. Somehow his head had fallen down to his chest, listening to his own train of thought about...something, something about being happy. As he looked up Simon was smiling at him still, standing there as if waiting...

Waiting for an answer.

James couldn't remember the question.

"You and I both want to help people, we want to lead people, am I right?" Simon prompted.

"Yes," said James.

"That's what life is all about. It's all really a popularity contest, isn't it?"

This conversation had turned into an argument of sorts, and James wasn't sure why. "I don't think that's what life is all about at all..."

Simon took a step toward him with his eyes were bright. "That is exactly what it's about, son. And I'm winning."

"No, you're not." James said.

Simon gave a short snort. "No? Did you just say I'm not winning?"

"Yes." James wasn't sure what tug-of-war game was going on here, but he needed to stay off Simon's side of the field. "I said exactly that. Now, I'm not really sure what's going on here, Simon, but I've got to leave now. I don't usually allow people to hang out in the church when I'm not around. So, if you don't mind..."

"You look here, priest," Simon growled, raising a finger.

"Priests..." James started to say, only to have his voice crack. He cleared his throat and started over. "Priests are part of the Catholic church. I'm a pastor. You know that."

Simon stopped, still with his hand in the air, mouth open to say something that never came out. Then he laughed. "Oh, you're good. I haven't had a challenge like you since I was down in Florida."

James gaped at the man. "What are you talking about?"

"Little town called St. Joseph. Ever been there?"

Simon stood between James and the door, so he had no choice but to remain calm.

"No?" Simon continued. "I suppose not. Of course you've missed your chance now, since everyone there is dead or moved on. The priest there, he thought he was winning too." Simon laughed again, and it echoed around the wood-paneled walls of the room. "You amuse me. I appreciate a challenge. This is going to be fun."

Surely he was witnessing Simon having a mental breakdown of some sort. James' hands started to shake. He shoved them in the pockets of his jeans to steady them just as Simon took a menacing step toward him. James held his ground. "I really don't have time for games, Simon."

"Yes, yes. You do. You have all the time in the world." Simon shook his head. "And I have more than that."

A dark, disturbing thought clouded James' mind.

Simon read it in his face and smiled. "Ah, Reverend. You've figured it out. You know what I am. I mean, what I really am! There's always one or two that can tell right off. But it took you a little longer..."

No. It couldn't be.

"Sure it can," Simon said, as if he could hear James' thoughts, standing there and tapping his foot with impatience. "Say it."

James didn't want to know, but he couldn't erase the answer once it came to him. "You... you are..."

"Come on, now. Say my name. Say it."

"You're nuts, that is what you are," James blurted out. "And I'm telling you to get out of my church right now."

Simon laughed long, hard and mockingly, but began backing down the aisle toward the double door. "You know what I am, priest! I'm here and I'm going to challenge you for the souls of this town!"

With those final words Simon spun around, his long coat swirling behind him, threw open the double door and was gone.

James listened as the doors slammed together with a loud and empty thud that echoed across the now empty church.

His heart raced.

He turned toward the giant cross hanging at the other side of the room and sank to his knees. "Dear Lord, please give me the strength to help this man for he seems to be truly disturbed. Let me protect the good people of this parish from his intents whatever they may be." James hesitated. "And, Lord, if he is who I think he may be..."

'Say my name,' Simon had said.

"Satan," James breathed now. "Lord, if he truly is Satan... I beg You for all the strength you can give. Amen."

CHAPTER ELEVEN

The clock above James' bedroom door ticked away the seconds.

He couldn't sleep.

He shifted from one side to his back and then to the other side.

His mind wouldn't let him sink into unconsciousness. How was he supposed to handle the situation with Simon? He'd never really dealt with someone under the influence of drugs or mentally ill and experiencing such delusions.

And the alternative—that Simon was telling the truth!

Was he out of his depth?

At five a.m., James finally gave up on sleep and took County Route 27 south about forty-five miles to a secluded spot where he liked to go when he needed to be alone. His head was cloudy from lack of sleep and a sandy scraping happened behind his eyelids every time he blinked.

As much as he loved his church and believed that fellowship and unity was the way to draw closer to God, sometimes he felt God's presence stronger in nature. God was the only one who could help him now. He needed to talk to Him alone.

Just past the neighboring town of Oak Falls was a brown and yellow wooden sign that marked his destination—*Oak Falls Wilderness Trail*. He parked his Jetta in the gravel lot on the side of the road and stepped out into the cool dawn, breathing in the scent of pine, and reveling in the silence. No one else was here this early, and that pleased him. He swung his backpack over his shoulder and headed to the trailhead.

The early morning breeze was refreshing. The pent up energy that had built up overnight blew away in thin strands as he crunched his way along a pine-needled trail through the shrubbery that lined the sloping hill. Recycled railroad ties demarked the edges of the trail, and a distant roaring reverberation dampened the sounds of small animals and birds awakening in the forest.

At a brisk walk it took him fifteen minutes to get to his favorite spot on the side of a hill where a rock outcropping looked out on a forty-foot wide, shallow waterfall, slightly too tall to be treated as a rapids, but that didn't stop the occasional daredevil from trying.

Vacant now, the waterfall was graceful and elegant—a determined strip of white and gray in an otherwise green countryside. It had a fairytale-like quality. But at the same time it wielded unfathomable strength, enduring time, wind and weather, crashing down without a doubt of its existence, without a question of its destination, into the water below.

It reminded James of his trust in God.

The rising sun warmed the skin on his face and thawed the solid block of fear that had lodged in his chest. The breeze caressed his skin, and the steady roar of the waterfall pounding against the rocks below was soothing.

From his backpack James pulled out a leather-bound journal that had somehow withstood the tests of time. He gently ran a hand over the front cover before he opened the book. It was smoothed over by the many other hands that had held it before him. Inside, the pages were old and yellowed, revealing a collection of prayers scribbled down in different handwriting styles.

His father had given it to him just before he was deployed to Kuwait to fight in Operation Dessert Storm. It had been in his family for generations, passed from father to son when the time was right, and it contained a prayer for almost any situation. James referred to it often. It was a gift to have the right words to turn to when he couldn't find the words himself.

He paged through the journal, skimming across

prayers until he found the one he was looking for and began to read. "Almighty and Merciful God, I come before You this early morning in the name of Jesus Christ, asking that You look upon me and hear me for His sake, for I am not worthy to ask anything from You for my own sake. O glorious Captain of my salvation, arm me for my conflict with Satan—for he is too cunning for me. O Lord, teach me his devices—for he is too mighty for me. You have destroyed the devil and his works. I believe in Your victory. Make me strong in the grace that is in You so that I may not fear evil. Send me out against him armed with Your invincible armor. Strengthen me O Lord that I fail not through the length or sharpness of battle, and enable me to persevere till You discharge me from the war. Thus, in a constant dependence upon You, would I fight the good fight of faith—keep up communion with You—and in every battle grow more acquainted with my wants and more thankful for every supply. O Lord, I humbly pray You hear my prayers for Thy mercy's sake. Amen."

James sat in silence for a few moments and took in the serenity.

"Lord, please show me my path."

He waited for an answer.

"Please, Lord. I'm not sure what to do."

Still no answer.

"I know this is a test, Lord, but I could use a little help."

As the sunlight broke through the trees and lit the waterfall like a sea of diamonds, it dawned on him. Why didn't he think of that before?

"Of course! Thank you Lord."

CHAPTER
TWELVE

Branson's reaction was calm and thoughtful, much to James' dismay. "Have you mentioned this to anyone else?"

"No."

"Keep it that way, you hear me?"

James blinked and shook his head. "But we have to do something. We have to help this town!"

Branson pursed his lips and nodded gravely. "Listen, James. You and I, we can talk about these things. We are men of the church. We know that God is real and that the devil is real. We can both agree on that. But you start telling people that Satan himself is walking the streets of our little town … they're going to think you're crazy."

"Maybe I am," James said. He slumped against the table and toyed with his glass of lemonade. Branson was right. The world in general might like to think there was a God out there, somewhere, looking down to help things along and intervene when it came time to pick lottery numbers, but the devil had gone out of fashion years ago.

"Okay, I understand all that." James set his glass aside and leaned in closer to his mentor. "But what do we do about this? This guy, this Simon Paradis, at the very least thinks he's the devil. He has spent the last week making friends with everyone in my parish and now he's going to go around trying to mess with people's lives. We've got to do something."

Branson leaned back in his chair. "Like what?"

James waved his hands helplessly. "What do you mean 'Like what?' We've got to warn people. We can't just sit back and do nothing!"

"What do you propose doing, James? You want to go at him all crosses blazing and holy water spraying? What are you going to show the members of your church? That you're a crazy man, that's what. This Simon is most likely just some poor old soul who has a drug problem."

"He didn't seem high."

"And you base that on what? Your years of experience with people with substance abuse issues?"

James looked at his friend and mentor, hurt. Branson's words hit him in the chest like a fist.

"I'm sorry," Branson quickly added when he realized what he'd implied. "I shouldn't have said that."

James held up his hand. "It's okay."

Nearly three years had passed, but the hysterical call from his mom asking him to come home was still fresh in his mind. When he rushed home from the university that night there were police cars in front of his house. Flashing red and blue lights painted the street in foreboding colors.

James ran inside and found his mother on the couch—her eyes were swollen and her face stained with mascara tears.

He still couldn't remember the sequence of events clearly. Everything had seemed like a movie being played at the wrong speed.

Drugs, the police had said.

Suicide.

His baby sister was dead.

What really struck him then, and to this day, was the realization that the last time he'd seen Julia, he hadn't even made an effort to say goodbye properly. She'd been getting ready for a party and was upset that he wouldn't give her any money. They'd argued briefly—an increasingly common occurrence in their relationship the last few months, and he'd waved a hand at her dismissively and left.

If only he'd taken the time to notice that she hadn't been okay. If only he'd recognized that something was wrong, that she was depressed, he might have been able to help her.

That was the moment he decided to follow in

Branson's footsteps and become a pastor. He wouldn't let another life slip through his fingers again. He wasn't strong enough to do it by himself, but through the Word of God he could help those who still had a chance.

That year James finished his last semester at the University of San Diego, and graduated with a heavy weight on his shoulders. Heavier than any young man at the start of his life should bear.

The San Diego County Crushers, Triple-A baseball team had offered him a two-year contract in the Pacific Coast Minor Leagues, but that kind of life, those kinds of dreams, suddenly seemed small. He wouldn't be able to make a difference playing baseball. He turned down the offer, moved to New York, and enrolled in Bible College.

James shook his head and tried to snap back to the present, to the problem at hand. "I'm telling you there's something not right about this guy."

"Son, I'm sure there is. But do you really think this guy might really be Satan? Ol' Scratch himself? Come to our little town in the middle of nowhere to do just what exactly? Mess with your mind? What did you do to attract that kind of attention?"

James turned his glass of lemonade, watching the condensation drops from the cool glass puddle on the table.

Branson leaned forward. "Listen son, the world is full of people who are messed up for all kinds of reasons. It's all part of the free will God gave us. Some of us follow

His Word, some of us worship another—like drugs, or money, or fame. Some of us are unbalanced and can't think right for some reason or another. Those are the ones that need our help. I think this Simon may be one of those. Help him, James. Don't fear him. You think this guy needs to be stopped? Then you stop him. But you do it quietly. No need to involve other folks in this."

"So how do I do that?"

Branson shrugged. "I'm sure we can figure it out, you and me. Let's start with this. Where's this guy staying?"

"I'm not sure… But he said he was going to dinner tonight at the Larsons…"

He glanced at the time on his phone. Just after five o'clock. Which meant Simon was probably there with Sally and Ben right now.

He looked at Branson, panicked. "I need to go…"

PART TWO

Be alert and of sober mind. Your enemy the devil prowls around like a roaring lion looking for someone to devour.

– 1 Peter 5:8 (NIV)

CHAPTER
THIRTEEN

James stood on the white washed porch and knocked repeatedly on the Larson's front door, trying to get a look in through the diamond shaped window.

"Just a moment," Sally Larson called out.

He released a breath he hadn't realized he was holding.

When the door opened, Sally stood there, smiling blankly. Her graying hair was neat as usual and she was dressed nicely. "Hello, Reverend Buchman. How are you tonight?" she asked. Her words were flat with no inflection in them. Her eyes looked at James but did not focus on him.

"I'm...fine, Sally. Thank you for asking. May I come in?"

"I'm really busy, Reverend," she said immediately, in

the same disinterested tone. "I have a lot to do for our guest. He's going to be renting our upstairs room. Isn't that wonderful? You have a good night now." And she started to shut the door.

"Sally, wait…" James said.

To his surprise she did wait, a hesitation that seemed to stretch her muscles as she tried shutting the door and holding it open at the same time.

"Uh, how is Ben?"

"Ben?" Sally asked, looking confused.

"Yes, Ben. Your husband."

"My husband?" Sally blinked and her eyes came into focus. "Oh, my, Reverend Buchman! When did you get here?"

He smiled, relief flushing through him. "Just now, Sally. Just now. May I come in?"

"Of course! It's so good to see you. What brings you by? Please, won't you come in?"

He stepped through the door, feeling he had won some small victory in a game whose rules he still didn't understand.

Sally led him inside to their living room. The space had always spoken to him of warmth and home. The two couches had red floral designs on them that matched the curtains. The fireplace was made of white bricks and was stacked with a few ceramic logs, meant for decoration and not for use. The rug was white and walls were a faint green. It was an inviting place to be.

The only blemish on the whole place was Simon, relaxing on one couch with his feet up on the Larson's coffee table and that same infuriating smile on his face.

"Hello, Reverend," Simon smiled smugly at him. "We certainly weren't expecting to see you here. I'm not sure if there's enough for dinner, is there Sally?"

Simon turned his gaze on Sally, who blinked as if she'd been touched by an unseen hand. Simon waited for her to say something.

So did James.

"Now, Mr. Paradis, I don't think it's very nice of you to speak to the Reverend like that," Sally said at last.

The look of pure surprise on Simon's face filled James with glee he was barely able to hide.

"And why do you have your feet on my coffee table?" Sally went on sternly. "Please, put your feet down. If you're going to stay here with us, you might want to show some proper manners!"

Simon turned slowly to James. His eyes were hard and his face was a complete mask.

He turned back to Sally before James could say anything. "I need to talk to you and your husband, Sally. Let's go find him."

Ben came into the room just then as if on cue, shuffling one foot in front of the other, his usually bright face looking tired and old. His balding head had beads of sweat on it.

"Hello, Ben," Simon said without turning around as

Ben came up behind the couch. "Please tell the Reverend that this dinner is just for us and he needs to go, won't you?"

"Ben?" Sally said to him, with worry in her voice at the sight of her husband's blank face.

"Reverend Buchman," Ben said in the same disinterested tone that Sally had used when she first opened the door. "I'm afraid I have to ask you—"

"To stay?" James said loudly, hoping he could break the spell Ben seemed to be under. "You want to ask me to stay?"

Ben blinked.

For a moment it had worked, he had beaten Simon at his own game and everything was going to be all right again and—

"There really isn't enough," Ben said flatly. "We're busy with our new guest. I need to ask you to leave, Reverend Buchman."

The words were like a punch in the gut.

Simon crossed his feet on the coffee table—an obvious act of defiance to Sally—and smirked at James. "It's easier with certain people, Reverend. Their minds are weaker." He waved a hand in front of Ben's face. "Old Jedi mind trick, you know."

Sally wasn't having any of it. "Ben, what is wrong with you?" She stepped around the couch ignoring Simon's glare and walked right up to Ben. She took his face in her hands. "Ben, look at me now. Look at me."

As Ben looked into the eyes of his wife, James saw him blinking in recognition. "Sally?" Ben asked in a small croak. "What...what's happening?"

"Mr. Paradis was just telling us that he has to go," Sally said, turning to glower at Simon.

Simon jumped to his feet, knocking a candy dish on the coffee table to the floor. He pointed a bony finger at James and said resentfully, "He's the one that needs to go!"

James stared at the finger Simon pointed in his direction. It was just a finger. Nothing scary about it. Nothing more than the outstretched pointer finger of a man of nondescript looks and an indeterminate age. It held no power.

All the power in the room was in the hands of Sally, being wielded by her love for Ben, a love granted by God.

"You heard the lady," James said to Simon with a sudden confidence buoyed by the sight of Ben and Sally hugging each other tightly. "It's time for you to go. Not just from this house but from this town."

"I like it here," Simon growled.

"Well, we don't like you here, Mr. Paradis," Sally said to him. "What on earth possessed us to say we'd rent you a room is beyond me. Shoo, now. Go on with you."

Simon didn't turn to her. His look of hatred and frustration was reserved exclusively for James. He kicked the corner of the coffee table and shoved it out of his way. As he walked past James he paused to whisper, "Don't think this is over, Reverend. We'll see each other again."

James knew that they would.

"Now, Reverend," Sally said, Ben still holding her in his arms and blinking every few seconds. "We made that hateful man a dinner, but I think we'd be much happier with your company. Would you like to join us?"

James smiled and tipped his head. "I'd like that a lot Sally. How are you feeling? Ben, how are you?"

Ben still looked a bit confused. "We're alright, I suppose."

Sally winked at him. "We're just right as rain Reverend, thank you for asking."

*　*　*

FROM OUTSIDE, A MAN in a tattered overcoat watched through the window as Sally, Ben, and James sat down to dinner. Simon Paradis, or rather the form that Satan had assumed for this little visit, was pleased. Things were progressing nicely.

Just as he had planned.

"Let the fun and games begin!" he said with a grin.

CHAPTER FOURTEEN

All through the rest of the week, James kept an eye out for Simon every day, expecting the man to pop up at any moment in that ratty old coat. He tried to find out where Simon was living but no one seemed to know. Everyone knew of the charismatic, eccentric man who had just moved into town. Most people had at least a few kind words to say about him. But no one seemed to really know where he came from or where he was living now.

As a new week began, James was exhausted. As a pastor he was prepared for his days to be full. Harmony might not have the big city rush that he remembered from his childhood growing up in San Diego but there were still a number of demands on his time here.

There were his usual duties of preparing for and

performing services at the church, and driving around to visit and check on the members of his community who were elderly or ill.

There were several charities that always needed help such as the Veterans Assistance Association and the Animal Shelter. Add to that the actual business of running a church and the hundred or so other little things he did from day to day—his life was already full and now it was getting fuller.

The primary issue now was that there were a lot more sick people to tend to. A number of people in Harmony were bedridden with a nasty flu bug, so many that the school had closed its doors last Thursday to give the kids a four-day weekend. The idea was to give everyone time to get over their illness before they brought it to school and spread it to others.

The COPs were out in full force. They were bringing soup and performing little errands for those who couldn't make it out of bed to do it themselves. James tried to go to a few houses every day where he knew people had contracted this virus, but it was becoming harder and harder to keep up with it, even with the added help of Branson and the volunteers from his church.

Something else had been nagging at James, too. Something that Simon told him—about that little town of St. Joseph in Florida. Simon had said it was gone, and implied he had something to do with it. At first James had just assumed it was an outright lie meant to scare him, the creation of a sick or drug-addled mind. But James had seen the way Simon seemed to manipulate people's minds, and that gave him cause to think there might be something to it.

There was one way to find out. And then James could get his focus back on the good people of this town, and off of the twisted fantasies of Simon Paradis.

CHAPTER FIFTEEN

In the middle of a busy Tuesday morning, James found a little time to stop at Harmony's library. It was a stout red brick building with tall, narrow windows, white trim, and flowers in neat plots outside. It was a cheery place in the middle of a typical fall day.

Sitting down at one of the four desktop computers available for the patrons of the library to use, James ran his hands through his hair impatiently. He usually used a computer to do paperwork and accounting for the church but little else. He preferred human interaction to cyber interaction and the simplicity and feel of paper to the jarring contrast of a computer monitor, but there was no faster way to do this sort of research. Logging on to the Internet, James typed into the search engine, St. Joseph Florida.

A list came up almost immediately, filled with church websites, and Wikipedia pages about Saint Joseph and Florida. More than ninety million results. Less than helpful!

He sat tapping the keyboard with a finger in thought and he barely noticed when Amy came in and sat at the computer across the table from him. When she cleared her throat he looked up, startled.

"Oh, Amy. Hi. I didn't see you come in." James kept his voice to a whisper even though there was no one else in the library.

She smiled at him in the way that women have for showing patience when a man says something foolish. She was in casual clothes, blue jeans and a comfortable blouse top. Her hair was out of its ponytail, long auburn tresses falling in gentle waves down her neck. He'd noticed, several times before, how pretty she was. He noticed it again, now.

He looked into her eyes, still embarrassed about his mental stumble last week. He was unsure of what to say next.

Funny, he could stand up in front of an entire congregation of people and give a lengthy sermon full of instruction and gentle criticism, but looking into Amy's eyes now James could hardly find the words.

The moment stretched and became awkward.

"How are things with Rick?" He settled on.

Her smile faded.

After a few moments, she started, "Rick and I..." There she stopped, took a deep breath, and started again. "I've finally decided that Rick and I are done for good. I just can't see myself being friends with somebody who can be that possessive. He only wants one thing. I can't take his pushing me to be what I'm not. I'm tired of his manipulations. The guilt trips. All of it. You were right. You were so, so right. All those times you told me that I should hold fast to who I was and cut it off completely with him."

"Amy, I never said you should end your friendship with Rick." His words sounded lame to his own ears. "I said you shouldn't give up your beliefs for someone else, true. I did say that."

"I know you didn't actually tell me to, but it was there for me to see, and you led me to it. You were right."

Had he been a little more persuasive than he had realized all those times he had talked to her? It had certainly been hard to not encourage her to leave Rick with the way he treated her. He couldn't say he was sorry to hear she had left him.

"Amy, I'm so sorry," was what he said. He was sorry for her, in a way. It hurt to end a friendship, no matter how bad that relationship was.

She shrugged and the smile returned. "It's for the best. I let him know that we couldn't have anything more to do with each other."

"How'd he take it?"

She snorted. "Not well. There were...things said that I wish I could un-hear. But he's out of my life now and I'm glad."

He reached out to put a hand over hers to offer her his comfort. Maybe, as a bit more than just her pastor.

She moved to tap at the keyboard in front of her, shifting her hand just out of reach. "Enough about Rick," she said. "What are you up to today, Reverend?"

James tapped the fingers of the hand he had reached toward Amy, wondering how to explain what he was doing without giving too much away. "I'm researching a small town in Florida. Well, a historical town, I guess. It's not on the maps anymore."

"Hmm. Sounds interesting," she said, pushing her computer keyboard aside to lean her elbows on the tabletop. "Having any luck?"

"Actually, no. I just started and I'm not really good at this sort of thing..."

"Okay. So...you're looking into the history of Florida?"

James returned his gaze to the computer screen and tapped a few keys. "Not the whole state. I'm just trying to find out about a little town that was called St. Joseph."

She came around to stand behind him. "I'm pretty good with computers. Maybe I can help."

He leaned to one side so that she could see the monitor in front of him. "See?" he said, pointing at the volume of information on the screen. "If it's there I can't find it for all of this other stuff."

"Have you tried doing an exact search?"

"An exact search?"

"Yeah. Let's try St. Joseph Florida in quotes." She leaned forward and typed in the search. "This should narrow your results."

Amy's hair brushed his cheek and James caught a whiff of her perfume, subtle and vaguely sweet.

"Is this what you were looking for?" she asked.

He forced his attention back to the search results. The first few websites listed were still of no use. One was a travel agency offering trips to scenic places in the state of Florida. Then, about halfway down the list was a link that read *The Mystery of St. Joseph.*

"Yes, I think so. I think that's it." He clicked on the link and the page loaded.

Tragedy Strikes! screamed the headline of a scanned newspaper from 1841. He read through the article slowly. The story was grim.

Four years before the area that would become Florida had been granted statehood, a plague had struck the port town of St. Joseph. Dozens of people died suddenly of a sickness that no one had ever seen the likes of before. Without warning, people began screaming in the streets. They bled from their mouths, noses and ears. Taken home to rest, they went into fever and convulsions and then died within hours. No one was safe as the disease hit all ages, the frail, the strong, men, women and children. There was no known cure. Within weeks, the newspaper reported, more than half the town's population had died. Many people had packed up and left, but the writer of the article said he feared for the safety of the rest of the territory if those persons carried the plague with them.

The tragedy continued as a hurricane hit later that year, leveling the church and most residences. Those who dared to rebuild were devastated weeks later when a fire swept through the town, burning every remaining house to the ground.

The article included horrific artist renderings of the town burning.

"Those poor people," Amy breathed.

Below was another drawing from further back in time. It was labeled The Founding of St. Joseph, and consisted of six men standing in an open field, shovels in hand, about to break ground for a building. They looked happy. They looked full of life. They looked—

James stared. One of the men was tall, with long dark hair to his shoulders, and a full beard.

Even in the grainy etching it was easy to recognize those familiar facial features.

Simon Paradis. Impossible, but there he was!

Aghast, James couldn't help but worry that the devil had something similar planned for Harmony.

Amy was squinting at the photo now. "That guy there looks familiar." She leaned in closer. "You know who he looks like?"

"Simon Paradis," James finished her thought.

"Weird. I wonder if he's related?" she said. Then she saw the look on James' face. "What's wrong?"

What's wrong? That was a question with a thousand different answers, all of which would only lead to more questions. Branson's admonition to not tell anyone about Simon's claim to be the devil came to mind. James didn't want to burden Amy with this. For now, he should keep this burden for himself.

"Nothing," he said, forcing a smile. "It's just weird. How do I print this?" he asked, hoping that would close the subject.

Amy leaned past him once more and typed the print command.

"Thank you for your help Amy. I couldn't have done this without you," James said, retrieving the pages from the printer.

"You're welcome, James. You know, the Internet isn't really that scary of a place..."

"You have no idea," he said, meaning every word.

Spontaneously, Amy reached out and hugged him.

James hugged her back, holding her for a moment longer than he needed to. A sense of strength flooded his body. He'd never felt that from any person before, certainly not from any of the girls he'd dated in college, not even Susannah, who he'd wanted to marry. This was something new. Something he knew was right.

She stepped back from him with a little smile and curled her hair back behind her ear.

"I should be going now," he said nervously. "I have a few more people to check on."

"I understand. A pastor's work is never done."

Not with the devil living in Harmony!

CHAPTER SIXTEEN

After checking on a few parishioners, James stopped at Ed's Diner for a late breakfast.

Ed's was an old-fashioned, mom-and-pop diner owned by Henry Caringi and his wife Pamela. Henry named the diner after his grandfather, a short order cook. They were famous for their home-cooked meals, American greasy spoon goodness, as James called them—a little taste of home. Inside, the atmosphere was reminiscent of the 1950's, with its black and white tile floor, long chrome-lined counter, round red leather cushioned stools, and booths that lined the walls.

James sat in a corner booth and read over the printouts from the library. He had more questions than answers and was beginning to feel a tinge of guilt. It really wasn't very Christian of him to be so suspicious of a newcomer in their community. Branson had a point—why, of all places on this earth, would the devil choose to walk around as a man in the little town of Harmony in upstate New York? It was much more likely that this man was mentally ill. Charming, manipulative and mentally ill.

"Reverend Buchman?"

James looked up to find Daniel Lapinski standing there, smiling.

"Daniel, good to see you." James said, pushing the printouts into a tidy stack. "Please sit down and join me!"

Daniel slid into the booth seat across from James. "Thank you, Reverend."

Just then, the waitress arrived with James' meal.

"Would you like something to eat?" James offered.

"Oh, no. I was just passing by and saw your car outside... I wanted to speak with you for a minute. Uncle Samuel says to tell you hello."

"Well, you tell him hello right back. He's been doing very well since you moved in to help him."

Daniel sat silent.

"So, what can I do for you?" James finally said.

"Actually, I was hoping I could maybe help you out. I've been doing odd jobs all around town."

"Yes, I've heard. You come highly recommended by my parishioners."

"It was great for the first week, but now it seems a lot of that work has dried up. I thought maybe the church could use a handyman? Or maybe you know someone in need of help? I don't ask for much in return, sir, just enough to get by on."

James smiled. There was actually a bit of restoration and repair work to do around the church that he hadn't been able to get to. It would be nice to have someone willing to do some of that work, and the church's funds could certainly afford a part-time handyman. "Well. I'm sure we can find something for you, Daniel. When could you start?"

"Today, actually." The young man ran a hand over the blond stubble on his chin.

"Well, first I'll have to clear it with the deacons, but I don't see why hiring you will be a problem. I've got a few errands I need to run this afternoon. Can you meet me at the church at three? I'll have a long list of chores for you, I promise."

"Great!" Daniel said. "Thank you so much!"

"You're quite welcome," James told him.

"How about me?" A familiar voice asked. "Am I welcome?"

Simon Paradis.

"Move over, Sonny," Simon said to Daniel.

"Actually, I've got things to do..." Daniel said, standing.

"I'm sure you do," Simon remarked.

"Enjoy your breakfast, Reverend," Daniel said as he slid out of the booth and hurried away.

"You know your problem, Reverend?" Simon said as

he helped himself to James' plate of eggs, bacon, toast, and hash browns.

"It's pretty clear yes," James said.

Simon speared a forkful of hash browns and stuffed it into his mouth, talking as he chewed, bits of food falling out. "Your problem is this…" The man swallowed and grinned. "You think too much."

There were bits of egg hanging in Simon's graying goatee. The long black coat he always wore was snugly in place, still frayed around the collar and cuffs. Actually it looked a little more worn and the fedora he wore over his long black hair looked scuffed and threadbare.

"You're looking a bit rundown there, Simon," James said to him.

Gutsy to trade insults. But even if in his soul he had a healthy fear of what this man was, God stood with him and he would not back down again.

Simon shrugged at his comment. "Nothing a healthy meal can't fix." He picked up a strip of bacon with his fingers and crunched down on it. "Needs ketchup," he mumbled. Picking the bottle up from the table he unscrewed the top and banged the bottom with the flat of his hand, making ketchup pour out all over the plate, soaking everything. "There. That's better."

James' stomach turned watching the man eat. It was like watching a trash compactor with a loose gear. "Simon, did you want something?"

"Yes, Coffee." Reaching over to James' side of the

table he picked up the cup that James had been drinking from and took a long swallow of it. "Ahh. Yuck. You don't use sugar? Cream? Anything? It's so...bitter."

James couldn't believe what had just happened. Had the devil actually stolen his breakfast and then his coffee? And complained about it? "I thought you had left town," James said.

"No, you didn't!" Simon shoveled in more food, ketchup blobbing at the corners of his mouth.

"Well. I was hoping you left, anyway."

"You know the thing about hope?" Simon asked. "Faith is the substance of things hoped for. Without faith, hope is... well, like an empty paper sack—light and easy to carry but absolutely useless. You give people faith to carry in that bag though and now they've got something that matters. Now they've got something that can make them dangerous. Because then, with that faith, they start believing they can do things."

"They can. People are capable of doing amazing things when they act on faith," James told him. It was one of the reasons he had accepted this job here, so far away from home. Faith had led him here—into a conflict with a man that thinks he's the devil.

"See, right there's what I'm talking about, Reverend." Simon pushed a strip of bacon into his mouth and then talked around it as he chewed. "You give people faith. The way you live your life, the way you talk to people gives them hope, faith and strength and...blah...blah...

blah. It's really quite annoying. I'm trying to do my work here and everywhere I turn, there you are." Simon's face twisted. "How am I supposed to get anything done?"

"You're not," James said flatly.

Simon took another pull from the coffee cup, winced at the bitter taste and offered the cup to James. James shook his head. "No, thank you."

Simon shrugged and finished off what was left in the cup. "Look. You're a good guy. I get that. You want to do good things. I get that too. I'm not that much different from you in that respect. It's just that what I think is good for people and what you think is good for people... they're two different things."

"Right. I want people to live. You want them to die."

"Not all of them," Simon said with a wave of his hand. "I need to keep a few around. The world would be pretty boring without people. But that's not my point."

"Then what is?" James could have stood up and just walked out. Should have, but he wanted to hear what this obviously disturbed man had to say. To know how to stop whatever scheme Simon was up to, he'd have to hear the man out.

"My point is this. You and I are opposing forces here in Harmony. I want one thing, you want another. It's just not working out. So I want you to leave."

James laughed. "I'm not going anywhere. Why don't you leave?"

Egg fell from the man's mouth as he smiled. "Because

I'm not done yet. It won't be much longer until I'm finished. I promise. Why don't you go on a vacation? Say, two weeks? Then come back. I promise you that if you leave for that long, when you come back I'll be gone."

"No," James said.

A shadow crossed over Simon's face and settled behind his eyes. "You keep saying that word to me, priest, and I'll have to cut your tongue out."

Ah. There was the devil's true nature. "No," James repeated, "I'm not leaving. No, you can't have this town for two weeks. Not two days, not two minutes. No."

The fork in Simon's hand was slowly bent double as he made a fist.

"Well, no matter," Simon said suddenly with a smile. "I tried. It's too bad about Amy, isn't it?"

James blinked.

"What about Amy?" he asked. He hated playing into Simon's hands, but if he was going to do anything to Amy...

"I just mean she was so looking forward to marrying you. Someday, I mean. In the future. Ah, the future you two would have had together! And now she'll be dead."

Anger rose in James, like bile burning up the back of his throat. "You will not lay a hand on her! You hear me Simon?"

Simon held up his hands, palms facing James, in a gesture of appeasement. "Not me. I won't lay a hand on anyone. But this whole town is going to die. I am offering you a way to save yourself and your new friend. But if you won't take it, she can die with the rest."

With a smile, Simon picked up the plate. And licked it clean.

Finished with his, or rather James', breakfast, Simon stood up and smoothed the worn lapels of his coat. "This is wearing a little thin, isn't it? Guess I should be done with it. Soon." He looked at James for a long moment and then tipped his hat, turned and walked away. "See you, priest."

If Simon was worried enough to try to bargain to get James to leave town, then he must see James as... what? Some kind of threat? A stumbling block to his plans? Whatever it was, James took heart from it. It was something to hold on to. However, he still didn't know what Simon was up to or actually capable of, other than wanting to hurt as many people here as he could.

Including Amy.

Leaving was not an option. He had to stay and stop Simon and save the people in Harmony from the devil's works. All of the people. Amy included.

CHAPTER SEVENTEEN

"**A**nd that's what he said?" Branson asked James, as they sat in Branson's comfortable office in the back of the church and shared lunch. It was a cozy space with dark wood paneling and a bright white rug. The furniture was heavy and the chairs were plush. James figured that because Branson had been here in town for more than twenty years now, ministering the faith to people, he'd had plenty of time to decorate.

"Why don't you go on a vacation? Say, two weeks? Just like that?" Branson continued.

"Yes, in exactly those words. I don't know what he has planned. But it's enough that he wants me gone while he does it."

"So, what do you think he's up to?" Branson asked, offering James another glass of lemonade.

"I don't really know. That's the thing that bothers me. He has a way of getting into people's minds. The way Ben and Sally looked at me—looked through me when he was there. And then those articles I found at the library. I'm worried. I have no clue what he could do. And here I am, walking around blind and unable to warn anyone because he's probably just insane and there's nothing to warn people about. I feel so frustrated. So useless." James had no appetite for the roast beef sandwich Branson had prepared.

"Maybe that's Simon's game, old friend," Branson suggested. "Maybe he's got some grudge against religious folks. Maybe he's looking for you to run around with your hands in the air screaming about how the devil's coming and everyone needs to get out. Cause a panic. Maybe he just wants to discredit you and make you look like a fool."

James peeled a piece of bread off his sandwich and chewed on it. Branson's suggestion made sense. There were people out there who had turned away from God and looked down on those who believed. Still... "I don't know. I get the impression that he really wants me out of the way for something."

"Okay, okay. But then, what?"

"Your guess is as good as mine." James leaned back and rubbed his eyes. "I've been so busy that I haven't had time to stop and think. The church, the community, I even had a guy this morning looking for work—"

James stopped suddenly and looked at the clock on

the wall. "Oh, no. Oh, Branson, I totally forgot. I need to get back to the church. I'm supposed to be meeting someone. Can we talk more about this later?"

"Of course," Branson stood with James and walked him to the door. "We'll figure this out, James. Don't worry."

James shook Branson's hand, but he be able to take his advice?

CHAPTER EIGHTEEN

James pulled in to the church parking lot just in time to see Daniel walking away, his hands stuffed deeply into his heavy green jacket. When Daniel saw James driving in, he stopped short.

"I was afraid that I was going to miss you," James said to Daniel, closing the car door behind him. "I'm sorry. I got caught up in a meeting."

Daniel shook his head. "It's okay, Reverend. I know you're a busy man. I'm not surprised you didn't have time for me."

Daniel's words were like a slap to the face. A gentle slap, but a slap just the same.

"Daniel, it's not like that, really. I told you I had errands. One of them was to get the okay from the deacons, and I did. We'd love to have your help around here. Let's go inside and we'll get started, okay?"

But Daniel was shaking his head before James even finished speaking. "Thanks, Reverend. But, I'm a busy man now too. While I was waiting here for you, someone else came up and offered me a job, starting right away. You don't have to worry about me anymore."

There was no mistaking the anger in Daniel's voice.

James said, "Well, I'm glad you found work, but I'm still sorry I was late." He reached out a hand to Daniel's shoulder.

Daniel jerked away. "Don't. I'm good, Reverend. Really. Don't worry about me."

He turned and walked briskly away, leaving James watching after him.

"Did you know," Simon said from James' elbow, "that if you spell devil backwards it spells out 'lived'?"

James jumped a little to have the man appear like that, even though he'd experienced it a couple of times now.

"So, the opposite of your name is a good thing?" James replied, not turning his eyes away from Daniel. "I'm pretty sure I already knew that."

Simon laughed out loud. "See, that's why I like you, Reverend! You actually stand up to me. It won't do you any good, but it's nice that you try. I'm so used to mealy-mouthed religious advisors who talk a good talk but then back down the minute I show up. You, you're something special."

James shook his head. "What are you doing here, Simon? I have work to do. That man down the street there needs my help."

Simon made a show of turning to see Daniel still walking away, and then turned back with that same predatory smile on his face. "No, Daniel is going to be fine. I asked him to do some more work for me, seeing how his local church couldn't help him out. Seems the Reverend was too busy with other things."

"You gave him work?"

"Oh, James, you really don't understand me at all, do you? I have so much a man like Daniel could do for me. Just like his uncle did, back in his younger days."

"Samuel? You know Samuel?"

"Oh, those were the times! Samuel Stirling and me, we were quite the team, in the day. Before he found religion and got all high and mighty on me." Simon turned his head, and spat on the front lawn of the church. "This boy could be quite the little helper for me. Like for instance, the front steps on my house are loose. I hear he does a real bang up job."

"Steps. That's what you came over here for?"

Simon just tapped his watch, smiled, then turned and walked away.

CHAPTER NINETEEN

Samuel hadn't attended services last Sunday and James suddenly couldn't help but wonder if everything was okay. He got in his car and drove over to check on him.

He was pleased to see that the mobile home had been freshly painted and the roof had been repaired. The lawn was tidy and some new begonias were in full bloom. A stack of lumber was in the driveway—most likely materials for the new front porch Daniel had promised. But still, something was out of place. Something didn't feel...right. Stepping out of the Jetta, he looked along the front of the house at the drawn drapes in the windows and at the newspaper still sitting out on the front porch waiting to be collected. He went up to the front door to knock.

No answer.

He knocked again. Then rang the bell. He could hear it buzzing from inside.

Still nothing.

"Samuel?" he called out. He tried to see through the window in the middle of the front door, but found a curtain drawn across that, too.

He tried the handle. It was unlocked.

Pushing the door inward he took a few steps inside. "Samuel?" he called again. "Samuel, it's me. It's Pastor Buchman. Are you home?"

A cough came from the living room. The smell of cigarette smoke filled the air. There were no lights on. With the drapes drawn it was difficult to see anything at all. What was usually a bright and sunny room was now a dark space. James saw vague shapes that had to be the couch, the older style bulky television on the entertainment stand and the rest of the furnishings. As his eyes adjusted to the dim light he spotted the recliner where Samuel was sitting.

The elderly man had his knees drawn up to his chest and his arms wrapped around them, rocking himself silently. James could just make out that the man was in pajama bottoms and a t-shirt. The faintly unpleasant aroma that told him Samuel hadn't bathed in a few days.

"Samuel?"

Samuel's head turned toward him. "Who's there?" he said in a weak, strained voice.

James approached Samuel and knelt by his chair. "Samuel, it's Pastor Buchman."

On the side table, next to the recliner, were seven lit cigarettes burning in a glass ashtray. James extinguished the cigarettes one by one. "Samuel, I thought you quit smoking? Is everything okay?"

Samuel laughed softly, in a sound with no mirth behind it. "No. Not okay. It's so dark out."

"Dark? Samuel, it's mid-afternoon. It's beautiful outside. The sun is out, the sky is clear. It's a nice, warm day. Why don't you let me open these curtains and we can talk about it, all right?"

"No!" Samuel protested, a slim hand reaching out to grab at James' shirt. "That is not the kind of dark I'm talking about."

James gently took Samuel's hand and held it. "Tell me what's happened, Samuel."

"Daniel's gone."

"Gone? I thought he was staying with you—"

"There's an evil in our town, Reverend!"

"Samuel," he said gently, "Samuel, what do you mean when you say there's evil in our town?"

The old man looked at him. James couldn't see his eyes in the gloom, but somehow he imagined they were wide and staring. "The devil. The devil's out there."

The words shocked James. He had never known Samuel's mind to be anything other than sharp. Was this a case of senility settling in? Well, the devil is in town, according to Simon. There was that small detail. But that wasn't something he could very well share with an old man already frightened out of his wits.

"What happened with Daniel, Samuel? Did he do something to make you afraid of him?"

"It's not his fault," said Samuel. "He's a nice boy. But he's messed up now."

James sighed. "A lot of soldiers come home troubled."

"He came home fine!" hissed Samuel. "But now he's got a new friend..."

James was startled at the sudden fury in the old man's voice. He stood and looked around the room. It was still tidy as usual, but he noticed the refreshment tray on the coffee table. It was set for three. "Samuel," he asked, picking up one of the cups and finding it cold to the touch, "was there someone else here to visit you?"

Samuel nodded his head a few times and pointed to the wall near the television. "Him."

James' brow creased in confusion and growing worry for Samuel. He liked this old man. During the time he'd served as pastor of New Hope Church, he had gotten to know Samuel pretty well. Sure, he had done some things as a young man that no one would be proud of—things that had sent him to prison for a number of years. But Samuel had done his time and come out a changed man, rededicating his life to God. The Samuel of today was nothing like the Samuel that had existed all those years ago.

As Samuel continued to point with a shaking finger at the wall, James got up and went to see what his friend could possibly want to show him. There was a row of pictures lined up and evenly spaced. Evenly spaced, except for the last one on the right. That one looked as though it had been hastily tacked up and whoever had done it hadn't cared about making it look right. Or maybe, they had wanted it to stand out.

In the dark room he couldn't see that last photo very well. It was an old black and white photo too, which didn't help. The one person in it was definitely Samuel, a younger Samuel, from back in the days when he was young and stupid. The other person looked to be tall, thin, dressed in black with long black hair and—

Oh, no!

James went quickly to the light switch and flicked it on, taking two steps back toward that photo before he realized the switch hadn't done anything. He tried it again, and again, as people do when they think for sure the next time it will make the light work. The bulb must be blown.

So to the windows he went, grabbing a handful of drapes.

"No wait," Samuel said in a feeble voice.

But James really, really needed some light in the room.

The curtains slid back with a loud squeal of metal rings scraping along the rod. Bright, slanting sunlight filled the room. Samuel covered his eyes with his arms and cringed as if the light were actually hurting him, breathing in short ragged breaths.

James couldn't tear his eyes away from the photograph. In it, standing next to the Samuel of the past, was Simon Paradis. With that same wide, predatory smile, same long black hair, same piercing eyes. The clothes were different, matching the period the photo was taken, but it was definitely him.

"How...?" he tried to ask before his throat closed up.

"I was a different man back then," Samuel's weak voice answered him. "You know that. You know what I did. You don't know...you don't know why. I had a friend. Thought I did. Thought he was my friend. He told me I had to do it. Told me it would make everything better. Told me a lot of things."

James watched as Samuel broke down and cried.

He knew what Samuel had done in his youth. They'd had a talk not long after James became his pastor. Samuel told him because he said confession helped his soul. He'd told James how he robbed a local coffee shop and accidentally shot a young waitress back when he was in his late twenties. Samuel was still with the waitress, sobbing hysterically over the injured woman, trying to stop the bleeding, when the police arrived.

Samuel had never told anyone about the friend who urged him to commit that horrible act. And now that friend had come back, all these many years later, looking not one day older, and had found him right here in Harmony. Had come into his home, sat down and had coffee with him. Now that friend had befriended his nephew, Daniel. And now Samuel knew the truth, just as James did.

Outside Satan walked the streets and Daniel walked with him.

Samuel had pulled all of his curtains shut, blocked out the world outside, and stayed here in his chair, afraid to face that truth.

James leaned down over his friend and took the man in his arms. "It's all right, Samuel. He can't hurt you. Not anymore. Not if you let the light in and trust in God."

Samuel grabbed onto James tightly and sobbed. "But Daniel...he doesn't trust in anyone right now..."

Daniel was the kind of person that Satan sought out, those who are most vulnerable and with his military training—the most dangerous.

"Then we'll have to find him and help him see the light."

※　※　※

JAMES COOKED SAMUEL A quick hot dinner while he showered and changed his clothes. When Samuel emerged clean and fresh for his meal, he looked around the living room, once again flooded with light, and even managed a smile. James promised to have COPs members stop in and check on him at least once a day.

It would take some time before Samuel got over his fear that the devil, now calling himself Simon Paradis, was going to do him harm.

James scowled. For all he knew, that was exactly what Simon had planned.

Why else would he make it a point to show himself to Samuel like that? It worried him that he had taken the trouble to befriend his nephew. Nothing good could come of that.

He drove back to the church and he focused his mind on his intent, on the request he had to make, and prayed, "Dear God, please watch over my friend Samuel Stirling. He hasn't always been a good man, Lord, we both know that. But he is a good man now, as is his nephew Daniel. I know that he is weak right now from his experiences in the war, but please protect him from the manipulations of the devil. The devil that is now, somehow really among us. I'd really love to know how that happened by the way, Lord, but I understand you may not be ready to tell me. If you could maybe give me just a few hints though, that would be greatly appreciated. Help me to stop Simon Paradis and to help those that he would otherwise hurt. Thank you, Lord. Amen."

CHAPTER
TWENTY

Another day passed and in the morning James was trying to clear away the mound of paperwork from his desk so that he could prepare for the COPs meeting. He sighed heavily and signed off on one completed form before starting on the next. Paperwork was one of the many things that were distracting him from figuring out what Simon's game was.

James signed his name at the bottom of the last sheet in his stack and stood up triumphantly. "Done. Finally." He glanced at the clock on the office wall. Twenty after nine. He should update Branson. He reached for the phone on the corner of his desk.

It rang just before he touched it.

He drew his hand back as if the ringing phone had tried to bite him and then shook his head at himself, feeling silly. Just a phone.

He picked up the receiver on the fourth ring. "Hello?"

"James?" Then silence.

"Branson?" His friend's voice sounded odd. Tired, maybe? Something. "Branson, what's the matter?"

"I need to see you. Right now," Branson told him, in that same flat tone.

"Uh, sure. Are you at your church?"

"That will be fine. See you here."

The line disconnected.

"Okay, that was weird." His brow furrowed. Well, no way to know what was going on until he met with Branson.

He locked the church behind him and went to his car. He never used to lock the church. It had always been something he had left open, in case someone from the community needed a place to go and pray or just think. Now he kept it locked whenever he wasn't there.

He turned out from the parking lot onto the street and then took a right turn toward Grace Community Church—Branson's church.

He was a few blocks away when he caught sight of Daniel walking down the sidewalk, a rucksack slung over his shoulder. That was something else he was going to have to set right. He had been so distracted that Simon had been able to swoop in and influence Daniel.

Maybe Branson was right. Maybe all Simon had hoped to accomplish with his little dialogue at the diner was get James distracted. Keep James from doing what he was supposed to do for the people around him. It merited serious consideration.

But he'd have to think on that later as he was already at Branson's church. He walked up to the metal frame doors with their triangular stained glass windows. Inside he found Branson coming down the hallway, a blue knit cap in place on his recently shaved head.

"Branson, what's wrong?" James asked.

"I'm sorry, I didn't get out of here faster but I had a few things to get done. So, what's up?" Branson said.

James was becoming more confused by the moment. "Branson, you called me."

Branson slowly reached up and took his cap off. "No. You called me, and said you needed my help."

The two friends looked at each other.

"We've been played," Branson said.

"Yes," James agreed. "He's trying to keep us occupied?"

Branson nodded. "He wanted to get us away from our churches... Only, I'm still at mine."

James was running out the front door and back to his car before Branson finished his sentence.

CHAPTER TWENTY-ONE

The Jetta skidded to a halt in the parking lot of his church. The building appeared to be fine. Just like he'd left it.

COPs members had already started to gather and were chatting among their cars. A couple of them waved at James.

He forced himself to remain calm and greeted Georgette. Together they went up to the front doors... and froze.

One of the doors was broken inward, the wood splintered right at the lock.

Someone was inside the church.

James snatched his cell phone out of his pocket to dial 9-1-1.

No signal.

He looked at Georgette who was doing the same.

She shook her head. She didn't have a signal either.

There was always good signal in the church. Always. Until now.

"Georgette, please go back to the parking lot and keep everyone away. Send someone for the police."

Her eyes were huge. "Reverend, you should come with me. Don't go in there alone…"

"I won't be alone," he assured her. "This is God's house."

Georgette looked frightened, but nodded and turned back to the parking lot where the other COPs were watching, unaware and unconcerned.

James said a silent prayer for protection and guidance and stepped inside, pushing the busted door aside as he went.

He moved cautiously into the narthex, into the sanctuary with its benches and its crosses on the wall. There, on the front pew, was something that made the hair on the back of his neck stand up.

A green rucksack. Daniel's pack.

The pack was open now, and empty.

"Daniel?" he called out. "Daniel, it's Pastor Buchman. I know you're here. Can we talk?"

"Oh, now you want to talk?" Daniel said from the back room, from his office. "It's a little late, isn't it, Reverend?"

"It's never too late," he answered, trying to sound conversational while quietly making his way to the door to his office. "Can you tell me why you're here?"

"Come on back. I'll tell you all about it."

James swallowed against a suddenly dry throat. He did not like the way this was going at all, but he had very little choice. Daniel obviously needed his help, somehow.

So, into his office he went. He found Daniel standing there. The man's face was white as a sheet, hair damp with sweat. In his hand he held a small device with a button on top. There was a sickening smile twisting his lips. His eyes were bright, as if he had a fever.

The device trailed a wire that led to what looked like a smartphone strapped to Daniel's chest, which was connected to multiple blocks of what he could only assume were plastic explosives.

The phone had a digital timer that read *02:47* and was counting down...

02:46...

02:45...

02:44...

"Did I ever tell you what I did in the Army before I was discharged?" Daniel asked him, his voice higher-pitched than it should have been. "I was a demolitions expert, a combat engineer. EOD Specialist. That's Explosive Ordinance Disposal, Reverend. Same as Uncle Samuel in World War II.

02:40...

"Uncle Samuel taught me more than a thing or two about explosives. I bet you didn't know that, did you? I guess you could say I followed in his footsteps. I blew things up. I was good at it, too. Real good. Until that accident that killed those two men. But that was not my fault!"

02:35...

It took a few moments for James' tongue to start working. "Okay, Daniel. What are you doing?"

Daniel laughed, in a strained and pitched tone. "Seriously? I figured that would be obvious. I'm going to blow this place up, you too, now that you're here."

"God," James prayed fervently, "I know you are with us. Help me. Help me help Daniel. Daniel, you don't want to do this."

"Yes I do, Reverend. You know why? Simon helped me figure it out. I haven't lived, that's why. I've done everything I could for God and my country and for everyone else but I haven't done anything for myself. I haven't lived! So now, I'm going to live. For one, shining moment, I'm going to live!"

02:18...

02:17...

He hadn't lived! The same words Simon used. Lived. It was 'devil' spelled backward.

James took one step closer to Daniel. "Daniel, I know you've had some bad things put into your head. You need to think for yourself again. What do you gain by destroying this church and me and yourself?"

The man raised the trigger mechanism. James raised

his hands in front of him and stepped back again.

"You don't get it, do you?" Daniel said, his face twitching now from the strain of holding his smile in place. "I'm not just going to kill you and me. I'm going to kill everyone! I'm everybody's handyman. People let me into their houses and their businesses. I have bombs all over town. Wireless technology. One of the things they taught me about in the Army. Didn't take me long to put them in. They all detonate off this timer. The timer gets to zero and the bombs go off. One goes off, they all go off."

01:58...

01:57...

"Hello? James?" a woman said from inside the church. No!

It was Amy.

"She's going to die too, priest," Daniel said in a voice that was definitely not his.

It was Simon's.

"Don't do this, Daniel, please," James begged him. "You don't want to do this. You're a good man. God loves you. The people of this town love you. You know that. Think, Daniel. Think about what you're doing."

Daniel blinked and his face relaxed for a mere fraction of a second, but then he was back in the grip of the influences that held him tight. "Going to blow it all to Hell!"

01:44...

01:43…

James had seen that momentary slip, where the evil that had closed around Daniel cracked and lost control. Just for a moment. Daniel could still be reached.

"Daniel," he said, speaking more firmly. "Daniel, look at me. Look at me, now."

Daniel did—his eyes were still bright and flat but they centered on James.

"Good. Good, now think. Who are you? Tell me your name."

Daniel growled at him.

Then he blinked.

And again.

"I…" he said. "I am… I mean…" Then he shook his head violently and pointed a finger at James. "Don't try to confuse me! I'm going to blow up everything! You can't stop me!"

"No, I can't, but you can and God can. You know you don't want to do this."

01:20…

01:19…

Amy picked that particular moment to come into the room. She looked from one of them to the other and back again before it registered with her what Daniel had strapped to his chest. She put both hands over her mouth and her eyes went wide.

"Amy, Amy, it's okay," James said to her, in a voice that he hoped was calm enough not to set Daniel off.

"Come over to me, Amy. Come and stand right behind me, okay?"

She nodded, her eyes riveted to Daniel, as she stepped over to him and stood there behind him. Not that his body would shield her from much, but it was the best he could do.

"Daniel," he said again, "you don't want to do this."

"Yes I do!"

"Is this what you came back to Harmony to do?"

Daniel opened his mouth, his jaw working, but no words came out.

"You're a man of honor and good intentions. Did you come here to kill people?"

"N-no," Daniel stuttered. "No, I...c-came home t-to start o-over. T-take care of Uncle Samuel. D-d-do things right."

"Good, good Daniel," James said to him. "That's right. Think. Think now."

Daniel bent over at the waist and put one of his hands to his head, the other one still holding tightly to the trigger device, but not pushing the button. Not yet. Thank you God, thank you.

00:59...

00:58...

"Lord, please give me the words I need," James whispered. "Daniel, I—"

"Shut up!" Daniel snarled, standing back up as if he'd been yanked on by invisible strings. He was jabbing his finger at James and yelling at the top of his lungs. "Shut up, shut up, shut up! You do not know anything! Nothing! I have not lived! I need to do this!"

"No, you don't," James said in a soft, gentle voice. "No, you don't."

Daniel blinked again, over and over. He lifted his hand and looked shocked to see the device there, the wire leading to his own body. "Oh, God... Help me!"

"Daniel. Shut it off. You can do it. You were a specialist. You can do it. You can end this. End it now, Daniel. You can do it."

Daniel's hands started to shake. James did not like that at all. He dared to step closer. "Daniel, it's hard to carry the heavy burdens life gives us. It's hard to see clearly and many times you just want to give up. But God is there for you Daniel. Ask and He will wipe away your tears of grief and sorrow, your discouragement, and all the sufferings."

Daniel's lips trembled. "What's happening to me?"

"Daniel, just let go. Cast all your cares to God."

Daniel was blinking so rapidly now that he was squeezing tears out of his eyes.

00:43...

00:42...

He was getting through to him. "Okay, good. Now Daniel, I need you to think. You know how to disarm the device, right?"

Daniel hesitated, but then he nodded.

"Daniel, focus. Can you do that for me now? Can you?"

Daniel reached a shaking hand toward the mess of wires coming from the timer.

Suddenly he screamed like a wild animal, dropped to the floor and began shaking all over.

James rushed to his side and grabbed at the hand holding the trigger and tried to pry it off the device. Either Daniel was convulsing too hard to unclench his fingers or he was fighting to still hold onto the mechanism. James didn't know which. But all he could do was hold tightly to Daniel's hand and hold his fingers off the button.

"Daniel!" James yelled. "Daniel, stop this! You have to disarm this bomb!"

"I can't!" Daniel cried out. "I can't! I want to, but...I...can't!"

"Then tell me what to do." The words were out of his mouth before he had a chance to think about what to say.

00:28...

00:27...

He had to wonder if these were the words he had asked God to give him.

"Blue wire! Pull...pull it out!" Daniel instructed him in that screechy voice.

James looked at the timer. There was a riot of colored wires, and two were blue.

"Which one?" he asked desperately.

"Striped one striped one striped one—"

Daniel continued to repeat his instructions while a vile chuckle bubbled up in his throat. James saw his eyes go flat again. And as he reached for the wire, Daniel tried to move his fingers over the trigger button.

00:21…

"No, no Daniel, no!" James was frantic now. He couldn't fight with Daniel, keep him from pushing the button, and disarm the device all at once. He couldn't do it.

00:18…

He'd lost.

00:17…

Daniel laughed hysterically. "Mine, priest! You, all of them, every single person in this town! Every petty human soul in this town is dead!"

00:14…

"God," James asked desperately, "what do I do now?"

00:13…

00:12…

00:11…

"What do I do?"

And then Amy was reaching in past him. She grabbed the striped blue wire and yanked on it violently.

00:09…

It snapped away from the timer.

The timer went black.

James was so surprised by what had just happened

that he loosened his grip on Daniel.

Daniel pulled away and got his finger on the trigger button. He pushed it, and pushed it again and again.

Daniel lay there, writhing on the floor, maniacally laughing pushing a button that no longer did anything.

CHAPTER
TWENTY · TWO

N ews helicopters buzzed overhead as patrol cars drove up and down the streets of Harmony. Officers using megaphones directed everyone to evacuate immediately. The Army's explosive ordnance disposal unit from nearby Fort Drum was already on their way with explosive-sniffing dogs to expedite the search.

Churches and school gymnasiums at the neighboring town of Oak Falls were preparing to provide temporary shelter for all Harmony residents.

Branson stood in the middle of the street, watching it all. He had called 9-1-1 from his church as soon as James had left.

Harmony police officers, J. Colmenero and A. Rodriguez, put a handcuffed Daniel into the back of a police car. He was oddly silent now. He didn't respond to any questions anyone asked him. He stared blankly at some invisible something directly in front of his face.

"Please God," James asked one more time, "help him. He didn't deserve this. Simon found some weakness in him and exploited it, I know that. You know that. Don't let him suffer for it."

Officer Colmenero turned to James and said, "You're going to need to evacuate with everyone else, Reverend. But before you go I needed to ask you again, did the guy say anything else about the other bombs? Where they were? Anything?"

James shook his head. "No, John. He's been doing handiwork all over town, so they could be anywhere. He just said that they were all operated wirelessly by that one device."

John Colmenero was a member of James' congregation. He was a good-natured man with graying hair and a serious outlook on life. He nodded as James answered him and said, "Anything else?"

James hesitated.

"What is it Reverend? Even the smallest detail could be helpful."

He couldn't come right out and say the devil put Daniel up to this, but he had to say something. At least point John in the right direction.

"You might want to talk to Simon Paradis, new guy in town."

John looked up from his notebook. "Do you think he is involved with this somehow?"

"I know Daniel was going to do some work for him," James said truthfully. Maybe John would be able to learn something he couldn't.

"We'll pay him a visit then. Guess we have our work cut out for us. By the way, nice job, both of you." He tipped his police cap to Amy who was standing next to James and then walked away to speak with a military crew that had just arrived on scene.

James noticed Branson as he walked up to a car driven by his wife. The men exchanged a long look that continued as he opened the door and got in. Branson nodded at James as the car pulled away, driving toward Oak Falls.

Amy touched James' arm. "We should leave now. They're going to need us to help organize things in Oak Falls."

He turned and looked at Amy. He had almost lost her today. He didn't know how much of the town Daniel had been prepared to kill, under Simon's influence, but he'd probably be dead—along with the rest of Harmony—had Amy not arrived when she did. "That was quick thinking back there, but why did you come inside?" he asked. "I told Georgette to keep everyone outside."

She cocked her head and looked at him curiously. "You sent me a text message asking me to meet you in your office."

He'd never sent that message, of course. He told her as much. She pulled out her phone with a little smirk to show him that she wasn't imagining things, but the message was gone.

James assured her that she wasn't going crazy and promised to one day explain. But now, they had to get out of Harmony with the rest of the townsfolk.

PART THREE

But evil men and impostors will grow worse and
worse, deceiving and being deceived.

— 2 Timothy 3:13 (NKJV)

CHAPTER TWENTY-THREE

It was forty-eight hours before the Army's disposal unit personnel were satisfied that they had located all of the radio-controlled-improvised-explosive-devices (RCIEDs) that Daniel had placed. Thirteen of them, not counting the one he had strapped to his own body, had been strategically placed in a circular configuration around the most populated parts of town—the library, the gas station on Elm Street, three different residences, the post office, the high school and at the park, near the merry-go-round.

That would have been enough to level most of the town as well as kill most of the people who lived here, all at the same time. It would have been just like the fire more than a century ago back in St. Joseph, Florida. James tried not to dwell on it. It made him sick to his stomach.

The police had questioned Simon Paradis and he, of course, had an alibi—having lunch across town with some new friends. There was nothing at all to tie him to Daniel's actions. The police saw him as a harmless man, new to the community and willing and eager to become part of it.

Could he really be reading the man wrong?

He was charming and manipulative, and then cold and calculating the next moment. A number of psychiatric disorders had similar symptoms!

Daniel himself had been turned over to the FBI, as trying to blow up a town was a federal offence. He hadn't spoken a word that made any sense since his arrest.

James was sitting in Ed's Diner again. Branson had joined him for breakfast. They were halfway through their plates of eggs and bacon when Simon sat down at table with them.

"Now isn't this nice?" he said to the two of them. His smile was less crooked and more mean-spirited this morning. James couldn't help but notice that the man's coat was more frayed than it had been. It was unraveling at both sleeves now. A hole had worn through at his right elbow.

"Leave," James said to him, firmly.

"You don't get to order me, priest," Simon said harshly.

"You know he's not a priest," Branson said, in a clear strong voice.

Simon gave a dismissive wave.

"It doesn't matter, Branson," James said. "Priest or pastor, I'll stand up to him and he knows it."

"Bah," Simon growled. "Whatever. I just wanted to have a little fun and you ruined it. Ruined it!"

James gaped at him. "Fun? You tried to kill us all."

"I did nothing of the sort. Not that anyone can prove, anyway." Simon shook a finger at James. "I'm just having some fun. It is kind of what I do." His face grew darker. "But every time I try to play a game lately, you kick my pieces over." Simon stood up, getting louder, grabbing the edge of the table. "This time, you flipped my whole game board over!"

He heaved the table over onto its side, sending dishes, silverware, food and little sugar packets flying everywhere. James and Branson sat still and Simon stood over them, heaving in breaths of air. He scrubbed the back of one hand across his mouth.

"What is going on here?" Henry Caringi stepped out from behind the counter, his large arms crossed over his chest, his face a mixture of worry and anger that someone would cause such a commotion in his restaurant.

Branson smiled at Henry. "Just a little accident, Henry. No big deal. Simon here was just leaving." He turned to Simon. "Weren't you?"

Simon scowled at everyone in the room and then turned back to James. "I'm done here." He turned with a swirl of his worn coat and walked to the door. He opened it, but before he walked out he turned around again, glanced at his watch, and locked eyes on James. "But this isn't the end."

CHAPTER TWENTY-FOUR

James began that Sunday's service by thanking his congregation for coming together as a community and helping one another during the bomb scare.

He gazed out at the people in attendance. They were listening intently to his words and looking at him with interest. With their full attention turned on him, he began his sermon.

"We hear a lot about Noah and the Great Flood these days. But how many of us remember the promise God made to Noah?" James asked.

"Today I want to talk to you about that promise. A promise we need to remind ourselves of during these trying times.

"After the Great Flood, the ark of Noah rested on

the mountain of Ararat, but Noah did not allow his family to leave right away. He kept them in the ark until God spoke to him and told him that the time had come for them to leave their refuge.

"To show his thanks, Noah built an altar and made an offering to God. And because God knew Noah's heart was pure, He was pleased with the sacrifice."

James paused and stared out at the faces in front of him. Nothing compared with being able to reach the people this way, to guide them with a simple life lesson wrapped in a story.

"In order to strengthen Noah's courage, and to make sure he knew that He was planning good things for him, God spoke to Noah. He said, never again will a great flood come to the earth. As a sign of His promise, God said that He set the rainbow in the sky. So when you see the multi-colored bow after a fall rain remember what God said to Noah in Genesis 9:13, '*I set My bow in the cloud, and it shall be a sign—*'"

James stopped mid sentence. Near the back, there was a particular face that had caught his attention. Someone he had hoped never to see again. Simon Paradis.

He picked up his story where he had left off, almost as if he had meant to pause there. "'*A sign of a covenant between Me and the earth.*'" It didn't seem like anyone had noticed, but James was distracted for the rest of the morning services.

He kept his eyes on Simon as much as he could through the service, right to the end. But all Simon did was smile benignly and nodded at everything James said.

CHAPTER
TWENTY - FIVE

After services, James stood at the exit as usual, shaking hands and wishing everyone a good day. A few people stopped to talk to him briefly and there were a few invitations to lunch, which were always appreciated. This time they made him feel a tinge of guilt. He was so fortunate to be loved in his community—and blessed that he didn't need to manipulate people to do it.

When the last of the parishioners had filed out, James walked back into the sanctuary of the church. He liked the simplicity. It spoke of humility and austerity. There was a cross made out of rough-cut two-by-fours hanging on the wall behind the altar and two smaller ones that hung on the walls in the nave, but no other decorations.

The skin at the back of James' neck tingled as he found Simon there, standing with his back to James, long black hair flowing over his collar and just touching his shoulders. He stood in front of the altar and looked up at the wooden cross on the wall.

"It's just two sticks of wood nailed together... Not even nice wood at that. Completely worthless, really. How can that have so much meaning for people?" he said to James without taking his eyes off the cross.

"It has little to do with what it's made of and everything to do with what it symbolizes," James answered.

Simon turned then and quirked an eyebrow. "Sacrifice..." he said.

"And love," James added.

Simon let out a loud laugh, clearly amused at the idea. "Right," he said. "Love."

"*For He so loved the world that He gave—*"

"Blah...blah...blah..." interrupted Simon. "I've heard it all before. Just have trouble grasping the whole concept."

James said, "I have some time to explain it if you like."

"Not at all," Simon said.

James took a wary step closer to Simon. "I'm surprised you're still here, Simon. There must be a reason. You seem a bit... conflicted?"

"Conflicted?" A loud snort of laughter escaped from Simon. "Now, that's rich!" he said. "I'm not conflicted at all, my boy. I know exactly what I need."

"Have you come to make a confession?"

Simon sneered and walked around James until they

were eye to eye. "You don't get to hear what I know, little man. Your tiny mind wouldn't get it. You can't handle the truth!" The last bit came out in a fair impression of Jack Nicholson's voice. Simon smiled as though he had made a great joke. He went to the front pew and sat himself down, his long dark coat swirling around him as he did. "I have no intention of leaving Harmony, my boy. And since you also insist on staying, I'm going to need a favor."

James nodded at him, trying to appear reasonable. "You're asking me for a favor?"

Simon spread his hands wide. "Why not? You are in the business of helping people, aren't you? It's what you do."

"I'm in the business of guiding people toward God. And away from who you claim to be."

The smile fell completely away from Simon's face and the scowl that replaced it was vile and full of hatred. "Don't go all high and mighty on me, priest. I was an angel before the filth of humanity first walked this mortal coil."

"I told you, I'm not a priest. I'm a pastor." James fought to keep his feet from backing him away from Simon but it was an effort of will to do so. If this man truly was insane he could be dangerous, but if he really was Satan, James doubted whether a few feet's distance would make much of a difference.

Simon waved a dismissive hand through the air. "Pastor, priest. What's the difference, in the long run?"

"Quite a bit, actually. Pastors can get married and have a family, for one," was his quick response.

There were at least a dozen other more important differences, but at the heart of it, the two really were more similar than different. So why had he chosen that one example to argue with?

Simon chuckled. "Well, well. Marriage and family, that makes all the difference in the world then, doesn't it Pastor? I know what's on your mind with your little friend Amy," he leered.

James' feelings for Amy were pure and he refused to let even Satan ruin it for him.

The man who might be the devil sat up straight and put his hands on his knees. "Look, I don't ask people for favors lightly. When I do, there's always a reason for it and always a good one."

"And always a price?" James guessed.

"Of course! Of course there is. I'm a businessman, after all. I need to get paid for what I do. But really, is God any different when He asks for something? You think the apostles didn't have to pay a price to be Jesus' little inner circle?"

James shook his head. "Are you comparing yourself to God?" That put the moment in perspective for him.

"I wouldn't dream of it," said Simon. "I am far more powerful. I'm here, aren't I? Where is He right now? You don't even have an effigy of him."

This might be Satan, with all the power and clout

that Hell gave him, or it might be just a very disagreeable man. Either way, Simon would only have power over him if he allowed.

And he wasn't about to allow it.

"Leave," he said to Simon, pointing at the double doors at the back of the church. "Now."

Simon's eyebrow rose. "You haven't even heard the favor…"

"The answer is no," James said. "To whatever it might be. Now leave!"

A wide smile slowly spread over Simon's lips and showed his teeth but his eyes stayed dark and blank. He stood up and took a step toward James. "I guess that's that, then," he said as he stepped past James towards the exit. When he got there he paused and said, "You know pastor, that there may come a moment in time when you regret not hearing me out."

James waited for the sound of the front door closing before he let out the breath he had been holding.

"I doubt it," he said. There was no way he'd regret turning away the devil.

CHAPTER
TWENTY - SIX

Four days passed and James hadn't seen anything of Simon and under other circumstances that might have let him relax. The problem was that the flu bug that hit town just over a week ago was spreading fast. He'd even heard of some people who were afflicted seriously enough to be hospitalized. The school closed its doors this morning to give the kids a four-day weekend. The idea was to give everyone time to get over their illness before they brought it to school and spread it to others.

By the end of each day, James was exhausted. He would go to ten homes a day and minister to the people there, with good deeds and kind words. This was a very nasty flu that was going around and it wasn't even flu season. No telling what the wintertime would be like, if this was any indication.

That town in Florida, that was no longer there, crossed his mind more than once. A sickness had wiped them out.

"Please God," he prayed, "don't let that happen here."

The only high point of the last few days had been the extra time he got to spend with Amy. She had taken a few days of vacation time to help him minister to the sick. Her presence was a little bit of God's light shining in dark times. His nightly prayers to God were not without a thank-you for that. Today she had to return to work.

A wave of satisfaction caressed James' heart as he pulled into the driveway of his little one-bedroom house, situated next door to his church. It was no longer just a house. It was no longer strange or temporary. It was really his home now.

The square house had a small porch in front, just big enough for a pair of rocking chairs and a small table. On the table were two bottles of grape soda. In one of the chairs, rocking patiently was Amy.

He shut the car door and took the four steps up to the porch two at a time. "Hi," he said with a smile, leaning against the porch railing.

"Hi, James," Amy answered with a smile of her own, leaning back in the chair. She had gotten over any shyness in using his first name. Since the bomb scare everything seemed easy between them. "Is it okay that I came over?"

she asked.

"My day's a little bit better now that you did, especially since you brought grape soda."

"Mm-hm. I know it's your favorite."

"Ah, you know me so well." He picked up one of the bottles and took a long sip. He had loved sharing a bottle with his father when he was a kid. When he had mentioned it to Amy in passing, she had surprised him the next day with a few bottles from the local store.

"Hard day?" she asked him.

"No more so than most," he said, which wasn't really an answer to her question.

"I'm sorry I couldn't come with you today, but I needed to get back to work. We've got so many people off now with this crazy flu."

"You've helped a lot this week, already," James said. "I'm glad that you were able to help as much as you did."

"They are saying they might have to shut the plant down next week if more people get sick."

James didn't know what to say. His mind kept going back to the old newspaper reports about Florida.

Amy continued. "I made a few calls. We've got all of the COPs out helping," she said. "Georgette Newman, Mary Feeney, Bob Morris, Simon Paradis..."

"Simon?" James said questioningly.

"He's been very helpful. Never seems to get tired..." her voice trailed off.

"Are you feeling OK?" James asked.

Amy didn't respond. She looked tired and a bit pale. "Amy?"

She fanned herself. "It's kind of warm out here..."

James had just been thinking that it was a bit cooler than usual. Worried, he leaned over and put his hand on her forehead. "You have a fever, Amy."

She nodded. "Guess I'm coming down with that bug, too."

"You need to get some rest."

"I think you're right," she said, and reached for her purse to get her car keys. Leaning over made her woozy and she sat back in the chair. "Wow..." she said.

"I'll drive you home," he offered

"But my car is here..." she protested weakly.

"We'll find someone to drive it to your place." He took her arm to help her stand. "I really think you need to get some rest, Amy."

She let him help her up and made it two steps before she fainted in his arms.

James carried Amy into his house and placed her on his couch with her head propped up on some pillows. He then got a cool cloth for her forehead. She was burning up and he couldn't rouse her. He had no other option than to call 9-1-1.

CHAPTER TWENTY-SEVEN

Amy came out of it just as the ambulance arrived, embarrassed and protesting that she would be fine, if they'd just take her home.

The lead paramedic took James aside to discuss the situation. "She has a fever and she's a bit dehydrated, but her lungs are clear. I think she'll be okay as long as she gets some fluids, and some bed rest. Over the counter meds will help with the fever. She lives here with you?"

"No," James said. "She just came over for a visit, but she lives in town. I can take her home and make sure she gets what she needs."

The paramedic looked at him. "She should have someone stay with her. If her fever gets any worse she needs to go to the hospital..."

"I'll find someone to stay with her," he promised.

"Fluids, bed rest, analgesic... Call us if her fever gets higher," said the paramedic.

James repeated the instructions and the paramedic seemed satisfied.

❊　❊　❊

AN HOUR LATER, AMY was safe in her own bed with Georgette from the COPs at her side. She had brought a pitcher of her special iced green tea with ginger and was preparing a pot of chicken soup in the kitchen. Knowing Amy was in capable hands, James headed to the pharmacy for the medication he promised the paramedics he'd provide.

The town had two pharmacies. James drove to the closest, a little family-run business with Falcone's written in neon above the front door. The owners, Philip and Melissa, weren't members of either his church or Branson's, but they were good, decent people. Philip was behind the front counter today. They exchanged greetings and James picked up a basket and went into the aisles to find the cold and flu section.

Mindy Ellison was there.

"Hi Mindy, I hope Jordon hasn't come down with the flu."

Mindy turned her head and James noticed that the woman's eyes were reddish. "No," she replied in a hoarse voice. "This is for me. Jordon and Richard are fine."

"I'm sorry you're feeling ill," said James.

"Me too," she said, although it sounded more like 'be too' with her stuffy nose. She held up several bottles of medication. "I'm trying to not let this slow me down."

"Well, I hope you feel better soon."

"Thanks," she said, and shuffled off toward the checkout counter.

James picked up a couple of different medications, not really sure which would be best. There were several brands and they each made the same claims on their labels. He was on his way back up to the counter, coming around the end of the aisle, when he bumped into someone. He was about to apologize when he looked up and saw who was standing there, with his smiling face and long dark coat with its frayed cuffs and collar.

The words died on his lips.

You don't apologize to the devil for standing in his way.

"Careful there, Reverend. Never know who you might run into." Simon gently pushed James back and made sure he had his balance before dusting off the front of his own coat and resettling his fedora.

"Simon," James said, taking two steps back. "Why are you still here?"

Simon lifted his arms and put a confused look on his face. "I live here. This is my home. You know how important home is, don't you, Reverend?"

What Simon said sounded familiar.

Harmony was his home now. He felt comfortable here, comfortable and welcome, welcome—

His thoughts were wandering again and it was Simon's influence. He shook his head to clear it. Why would the devil feel it necessary to take human form and walk the streets of Harmony plotting and scheming?

"Sure you won't reconsider that favor, Reverend?"

A rush of anger rose inside of James. "What are you doing here, really?"

The devil in the guise of a man smiled at James. "Nasty flu going around, you know. I came down here to get some medicine for a few friends. Just like you did." He pointed at the bottles in James' basket. "For Amy?"

His words would have sounded sincere if not for that smile.

And then he turned and walked toward the front of the store, saying goodbye to Philip on his way past.

James stared after him and then walked to the front counter and put his selected medicine bottles down for Philip.

"Nice guy, that Simon," Philip said.

James wasn't sure he'd heard Philip right. "You know him?"

"Oh, sure, he came over to the house just last

week. Seems he moved into a house a few places down from us and he wanted to introduce himself. Nice man. We had supper together a couple of times. Haven't been able to get together since, though. My wife's taken sick with this flu that everyone's got. She has asthma, you know, so it hit her pretty hard. Took her to emergency last night."

"Oh, I'm sorry to hear that, Philip. Anything I can do?"

"Nothing you can do, Reverend. Except pray for her, I guess. I'll be shutting the store down early to head over there..."

James promised to pray for Melissa and then stepped out of the store into the early evening sunset. It would be dark soon enough.

Getting back in his car, he started the engine and headed back home.

Simon had claimed he was concerned for the sick people of Harmony—James doubted that seriously.

What if...

The traffic light ahead turned red and he had to brake hard for it.

The idea was crazy.

There was no way a mere man had that kind of power.

The green light came and it wasn't until the car behind him honked that James realized he was supposed to drive through.

He needed to talk to his friend and confidant, Branson.

But first, he needed to get this medicine to Amy.

CHAPTER
TWENTY-EIGHT

Georgette answered Amy's door. The tiny apartment was filled with the aroma of garlicky chicken soup. James' stomach growled in hunger and Georgette smiled.

"There's plenty," she said, taking the bag of medications from his hands. "Help yourself to a bowl."

"Thanks, but I want to see Amy first. How is she doing?"

"I feel terrible," a voice called from the bedroom.

James peeked in the door and saw Amy sitting up in bed with a blanket wrapped around her shoulders, her face a little green around the edges and her eyes red.

"You look terrible," he confirmed.

"Oh, thanks." She coughed. "Just what every girl wants to hear."

He laughed and entered the room, sitting on the edge of her bed. "Poor Amy. You going to be all right?"

She rolled her eyes. "It's just the flu, James. I'll be—" another cough, "—fine."

"Mm-hmm," said Georgette, approaching the bed with a bottle and a spoon. "What you'll be is on bed rest."

Amy shook her head, which amounted to her rolling it from side to side while she rested against the pillows. "Gotta work tomorrow."

"I think they'll understand if you call in sick," James said. "I'll write you a note, if you like."

"I don't know if a note from a pastor is as good as a note from a doctor..."

James feigned offense. "It should be!"

Amy gave a short laugh, which turned into a cough. She swallowed and her eyes closed—in general she just looked miserable.

"Here," Georgette said, leaning over with a spoonful of bright orange-tinted medicine. "This will make you feel better."

"Are you sure? It smells terrible!" Amy said.

James agreed. It was a strong smell full of menthol and camphor—different from any cold or flu medicine he'd smelled before.

"Medicine is supposed to smell terrible," Georgette said. "Now open..."

A thought occurred to James. A memory of Simon being in the pharmacy with him today, and of something he had said.'I came down here to get some medicine for a few friends.' But when Simon had left, he hadn't bought any medicine.

"Wait," said James. "Where did you get that?" he asked Georgette.

"From the bag you brought."

"Don't give her that..."

"Why on earth not?"

"I... I don't think it covers all of her symptoms," he said, scrambling for an answer. "I bought more than one type..." James took the bottle and the spoon away from a bewildered Georgette and walked quickly into the kitchen where the bag of medicine lay on the table. He screwed the lid back onto the bottle he had taken from Georgette. A greenish slime swirled inside the orange liquid like worms. James took the other two bottles out of the bag and held them up to the light. Nothing offensive swirled in either one and both were well-known brands.

"What are you looking at?" Georgette said from behind him.

"The labels," James said quickly. He offered her one of the new bottles. "I think this one is more suitable, don't you?"

She took it from his hand and said, "If you say so..." She returned to Amy's bedside with the new bottle and a new spoon.

Alone, James examined the bottle with the swirls inside. S'Wellness...it wasn't a brand he was familiar with, but other than that it looked like any other medicine bottle. It promised relief from various cold and flu symptoms, had dosing information on the side, and had the same kind of white twist-top that the other bottle had.

It was just a bottle. Nothing else.

He reached a finger out to it. Slowly, he got closer and closer to the side.

The bottle turned as he did, the e's in the brand name suddenly resembling an animal's eyes, watching his hand.

Okay, that wasn't normal.

"God," he prayed, on impulse. "I don't know what this is. But I'm sure it has something to do with Simon. It has something to do with my friends and neighbors, Your children, getting sick. I know what happened to that town in Florida. Is he here to do it again? Please, Lord, help me to know what to do here."

James put the foul medicine bottle back in the paper bag and walked into Amy's bedroom just as her phone rang. Instinctively, she retrieved it from the nightstand and looked at the number. She grimaced, looked up at James and said, "Rick."

"Go ahead," he told her.

Amy pressed the answer key and said, "Hello." Then she shook her head. "No. I can't. No, Rick, listen to me. I'm sick. I'm not coming over there. You've got to calm down." Her eyes closed and she shouted into the phone, "Rick, please. Don't. Don't do anything stupid!" There was an alarm in her voice.

"Amy. Give me the phone."

She hesitated for a few heartbeats, looking at him with her bottom lip caught between her teeth. Then she handed him the phone.

"Rick?" he said. "Rick, this is Pastor Buchman."

At first all James could hear was muffled sobbing on the other end of the line. "You? I don't want to talk to you," Rick finally said. "I want to talk to Amy. Put Amy back on the phone."

"She doesn't want to speak with you right now. She's not feeling well. Maybe, once you have your head in the right place, the three of us can sit down and discuss things. But not now."

The look of gratitude Amy gave him warmed his heart and broke it, both at once.

The tone of Rick's voice changed from grief to anger. "You think you're so much better than me?" He snarled. "Do you? Do you? Don't go all high and mighty on me, priest."

James stopped breathing. Those were Somon's words.

"Rick, is someone there with you?" he asked when he could breathe again.

There were muffled sounds and whispered voices, as though the phone were being handed off to someone else. Then a familiar voice spoke to him.

"Hello, Reverend," Simon said. "Having a nice visit with poor Amy?"

James' mouth was suddenly dry and he had to swallow several times before he trusted his tongue to work. "What are you doing there?"

Simon chuckled, in a low and vile sound. "I told you that you should have done me that favor."

"Let me talk to Rick."

"I'm afraid that won't be possible, not for you, or anyone else shortly."

The phone went silent.

James set it down on the nightstand, his mind racing.

"James, what's wrong? Who was there with Rick?" Amy asked him. He could hear the worry in her voice.

"Where would Rick be, right now?"

"At work or his house. You know the place? Over on Third Avenue?"

He did.

"Georgette, will you be staying with Amy?"

"Yes, I'm spending the night."

"Good, I feel better knowing that she is in good hands."

"James, what's going on?" Amy asked. "You're scaring me."

"Everything will be fine. I promise."

But as he got into his car and drove off, well over the posted speed limit, he wasn't so sure.

CHAPTER
TWENTY-NINE

Rick's house was a duplex really, but the other side had been vacant for a few years, and Rick was the only tenant. It was on a street full of similar-looking houses, some of which had also been turned into apartments, and some were still houses unto themselves. The one Rick lived in was painted a horrible shade of yellow with red trim. James went up to the front door and knocked. It swung open slowly when he did.

Crying and mumbling came from inside. Cautiously he entered, walking softly, trying to see all around him at once.

The kitchen door was open. Dirty dishes were piled in the sink. Empty frozen food wrappers were scattered across the counter tops. A half-eaten bowl of cereal was on the small round table.

The next room was the living room. The two windows had blue striped sheets instead of curtains nailed to the wall on either side. The carpet was dirty and littered with crumpled soda cans. A broken-down green couch and a pink recliner with yellow flowers on it were the only pieces of furniture other than an entertainment center with a large-screen plasma television and tall speakers that took up most of one wall. It was still on some police drama, flashing lights and racing cars making chaotic visual images with the sound muted.

And Rick had wanted Amy to move into here with him? James sent that thought back into the corner of his mind from where it had come. It was kind of irrelevant at the moment.

The crying was coming from down the hallway that led off the living room, from a room that had its door closed. James went up to it and pushed. This door, too, swung open.

It opened onto a bedroom with a dark blue rug and walls painted black and a bed with black sheets on it. Black sheets were also tacked up over the window, but had come loose on one side. Dust floated in the beam of light from the street lamp outside. On the bed sat Rick wearing nothing but a pair of boxer shorts. His muscular arms were shaking as he held a razor blade in his right hand and stroked it gently against his left wrist.

"Rick," James spoke softly.

Rick's pale skin stood out in stark contrast to the

dark sheets he sat on. He looked up at James with tears blurring his eyes. "Go away! Just leave me alone! I want Amy back. I want her back..."

The razor blade hovered over Rick's wrist.

"I know, Rick, I understand—" James tried.

"No you don't!" Rick screamed at him. "How can you know? Huh? She wasn't your girl, she was mine! She was."

"She still is," a low voice spoke from the corner behind James.

James turned and saw Simon. In his black clothing it was hard to see him at first, against the dark walls in the dark room.

"She is still your girl," Simon said. "You need to show her how much you love her. How badly you need her. It's the only way to get her back."

James saw Rick's face go slack even as his mouth reformed the same words. "She still is my girl. This will get her back."

"Rick! Snap out of it!" James yelled as loudly as he could. Rick's head whipped up and just for a moment his eyes focused on James. "That's right, that's right Rick. Look at what you're doing. Look." He pointed to Rick's hands.

Rick looked down and saw the razor blade between his thumb and first finger. He turned it over to stare at it as if he didn't know how it had gotten in his hand.

"Don't listen to him, Rick," Simon whispered through

his teeth, his smile broad and knowing. "This is what a man does. He takes control of the situation. If she can't see how much you love her, then you show her."

"I... I'm going to show her," Rick mumbled, and moved the blade back.

James stepped over to the bed and sat down next to Rick. He covered the hand with the razor blade. "Give that to me, Rick."

Rick looked at him, his eye like a child's. "But I love her."

"I know. I know you do. But doing this isn't the way to show her. You're only going to scare her."

He blinked at James. "I don't want to scare her. I wouldn't want that. I... I love her, you know?"

"I know, Rick." James carefully took the blade from Rick's fingers and carefully slipped it into his own pocket.

Simon took two long steps across the room and yelled in Rick's face, "He doesn't want to help you! He wants Amy for himself, you stupid, ignorant human!"

Rick's face changed in an instant, going from stupefied calm to irrational rage as he stood up. "Is that it? Well, you can't have her!" He lunged at James, fists at the ready.

James ducked the first of Rick's swings and backed out of the bedroom doorway as Rick stumbled after him, walking like a drunken man under water. Despite his obvious fury he was slow, as if his own body was struggling for control.

"Rick, listen to me!" James held his hands up with

the palms out, trying to calm Rick down again. "You don't want to do this!"

Simon followed Rick, magically staying just far enough out of swinging range. "Yes you do," he hissed.

"Yes I do!" Rick screeched, spittle flying.

"You see, Reverend," Simon spoke to James over the sound of Rick huffing and groaning like a heavyweight boxer in a title match, "here's the thing...simple minds like Rick's here are easy to influence. Whisper the right words, and he will do anything I say." Simon directed his words to Rick. "He is taking Amy from you. You have to break his neck."

"Break his neck," Rick grated from between clenched teeth.

"See?" Simon grinned. "Rick is an unstable, violent individual. It doesn't take much to push him over the edge. He might very well have got to this point on his own, without my influence. But I couldn't rely on it, and this way is more fun." Again, Simon spoke directly to Rick. "Amy is cheating on you with this pitiful little man..."

"Arrrggh!" Rick growled furiously.

"No, that's not true," James said.

"You know it's true, Rick. You have to kill him and Amy too!"

"No!" shouted James. "You don't want to hurt Amy!"

"Hurt... Amy!" Rick groaned.

James could see that. Rick was steadier on his feet

now, stepping faster, less at war with himself and more certain of his hateful intent.

Simon chuckled. "I don't think he wants to listen to you anymore, Reverend."

James tripped over the leg of one of the three chairs around the small kitchen table and fell backward onto the floor. He landed badly, the wind knocked out of him.

Rick took the opportunity to pick up one of the knives from the kitchen counter.

James raised an arm up for protection and started scrambling backward toward the front door.

Rick followed, swinging the knife wildly.

The blade grazed James' forearm and he cried out in pain.

Rick swung the knife back around faster than James could anticipate. The blade sliced deep into his shoulder.

James tried desperately to get to his feet, but Rick lunged and knocked him back to the floor.

This time the blade penetrated his stomach.

He fought back, grabbing Rick's arm, and tried to prevent the knife from plunging any deeper.

The air grew thick with the smells of Rick's musk cologne, sweat, and a strange metal odor, he couldn't quite identify.

"Gonna kill you!" Rick screamed.

Weakened from blood loss, James' arms threatened to fold as he held the madman back. His vision blurred and began to grow dim.

Suddenly, Rick's weight was lifted off of him. James shook his head to bring back his focus and saw two men in uniform forcing Rick to the floor. "Police! Stop resisting!" one of them yelled out loudly as Rick continued to thrash and try to get up.

One of them kicked the knife from Rick's hand and together they restrained him with handcuffs.

"Gonna kill you! Gonna kill Amy!" Rick said, over and over.

When he looked back into the living room, Simon was gone.

CHAPTER THIRTY

James lay on a gurney outside of Rick's house while Officer Anthony Rodriguez finished taking down his statement.

"We've got to get him to the hospital," the paramedic interrupted.

The officer nodded. "You're lucky your friend Amy made the call, you know."

"I do," James said.

"I don't know what kind of drugs this guy was on, but he was certainly gaining the upper hand."

They probably wouldn't find any drugs when Rick was tested.

"I'll thank her as soon as I see her again," James said, and watched as Officer Rodriguez and Officer Colmenero placed Rick in the back of their patrol car and then drove off, hopefully taking him to the hospital where he could get the mental health services that he needed. Needed even more so now that the devil had messed with his mind.

"I only pushed him a little, you know," Simon said, suddenly at James' elbow. "Everything he did, he had already been thinking about doing before I came along."

"Why don't I believe that?"

"Because you think everything I say is a lie. It's not, you know. I wasn't lying when I said I needed a favor."

"And what favor exactly, did you think I would do for you?"

"Why, I was going to ask you to talk to Amy and have her stay with Rick. You know he wouldn't have tried to kill himself if she'd only just stayed with him. But no, you had to go and make a play of your own for her. This is really all your fault, isn't it?" Simon smiled.

James tried to push himself up on the gurney with his elbows, but the pain in his stomach was too intense. "I would never push Amy into a life of mental abuse with that man."

"Because you love her."

He was blindsided by Simon's words, which took the momentum out of his argument. He blinked. Why had those simple words stopped him so completely?

"Sir," one of the paramedics interrupted. "We need to take our patient now."

"By all means," Simon smiled and backed away. "My work here is almost done."

CHAPTER THIRTY - ONE

As the ambulance raced through the streets of Harmony, sirens blaring, the paramedics fought to keep James calm. He thrashed around on the gurney, desperate to break free. As they tried to keep him still, James looked from one to the other and struggled more furiously than before. They both looked eerily like Simon, their lips curved into his unmistakable evil grin.

"No, I won't let you hurt any more of my people, Satan. I will fight you until my last dying breath."

The taller of the two paramedics leaned in closer and looked him in the eye. He took his hand and everything came into focus. His name tag read *V. Darrell* and he didn't look like Simon at all.

"Don't worry, nothing is going to get you in here. You're perfectly safe."

After glancing at the other paramedic to be sure Simon wasn't still with them somehow, James relaxed into the gurney. He was drenched in sweat and started to shiver. He took a deep breath and closed his eyes.

"Sir? I need to keep your eyes open for me, please."

James had been injured before, but this was nothing like the times he'd broken bones or torn muscles playing baseball. This was much worse. The pain that radiated from his stomach was unlike anything he'd ever felt. Something was terribly wrong with him. His hands and arms ached and stung where he had been cut.

The ambulance stopped abruptly in front of the tall glass-fronted emergency room at Harmony Memorial. The back doors flew open, and red, blue, and white lights flashed all around. James grew nervous when he heard other voices, worried that Simon could be near. He tried to sit up and immediately regretted it.

"Sir, you're hurt pretty bad. Don't move, okay?"

They rolled him through the automatic doors and into chaos.

Now there were a few more faces staring down at him, and he scanned their faces in turn. They were chattering and shouting to each other, and none of them were smiling, evilly or otherwise.

James tried to glance around and saw other patients lined up in the hall. Spots appeared as his eyes adjusted to the blinding glow of the florescent lights. Nurses were buzzing around administering IVs. The paramedics were talking to the doctors as he was rolled into a tiny stall made of curtains.

The curtains did little to dim the sound of the commotion of the bustling ER. Phones were ringing and people were yelling and crying. One woman was screaming awfully loud about the pain she was in. All the sounds combined into a shrill buzz that hurt his ears. It was like the time when he was eight and he and a friend set off a cherry bomb. Their ears had rung for hours. He pulled himself together and focused on the voice nearest to him.

"What've we got?" asked the attending physician, looking out from under a pair of bushy brown eyebrows. He wore a blue head covering, but James could see the end of a ponytail jutting from the back.

"Stab wound to the abdomen, defensive wounds to the hands and forearms. Patient's name is James Buchman. He's the new Reverend over at New Hope Church. Patient was hallucinating."

James wanted to protest, but he had been seeing things that weren't really there.

"Hallucinating?" the doctor asked.

"Says the devil is coming to get him."

"That's the second one this week."

Second one this week? James' heart skipped a beat. Had Simon revealed himself to others? Could others see his true nature?

"Let's get a sonogram to check his wounds. Nurse,

run a tox-screen. Reverend, my name is Doctor Berteli and this is Nurse Kramer. We're going to take good care of you. I'm going to push on your stomach now, okay?"

James blinked and nodded. The doctor pressed up under his rib cage and then worked his way inward. James winced when he probed with his fingers near the wound. It almost felt like being stabbed again. He fought back a wave of nausea.

"Reverend," Dr. Berteli continued, "We need to find out if the knife penetrated the abdominal wall and if you have any internal bleeding before we patch you up. Any allergies we should be aware of?"

He shook his head. His mouth was dry and he didn't trust himself to speak.

"I'm going to start an IV," said Nurse Kramer, as she inserted a needle into his arm.

He managed a weak smile and a nod.

A new voice was shouting. James lifted his head slightly to investigate and saw a doctor at the nurse's desk yelling into the phone.

"We need someone here now! Not tomorrow, now! This is no ordinary flu!"

"The...devil is to blame..." James blurted out. "He brings pestilence and death with him. The devil is to blame!"

"Nurse, get Mr. Buchman a sedative. And put a rush on that tox-screen. I need to see what we're dealing with here."

James tried to brush Nurse Kramer's hand away from the IV port. He needed his wits about him, not a sedative.

"Please, listen to me. This is what he wants, he wants me to be too weak to fight."

"Sir, you need to rest now. This medicine will help you do that." She deftly inserted the needle and pressed the plunger.

"No," James whispered.

The medicine.

Even while the sedative took effect, James made the connection.

The S'Wellens medicine. He was certain of it.

Before he could tell anyone his theory, the sedative took full effect. They probably wouldn't believe him anyway.

Darkness swirled around him and swallowed him as he lost consciousness.

CHAPTER THIRTY - TWO

"James, you're a good man, and I'm proud of you, but this battle that you're fighting is far from over." The voice was one James never expected to hear again. "He has to be stopped. He fears you, James. Only you can stop him."

The voice was that of his father, but his father was dead. He must be dreaming, and the voice a product of his imagination, or the medication, but those words still struck a chord.

God was using the voice of his father to send him a message.

"What can I do?" James asked. "Please, give me a sign. I am Your instrument. I will do Your work in Your name."

He saw bright flashes of people dying from the illness spreading through his community...

Flashes of his church...

Flashes of the garden behind the church...

Flashes of Simon...

Flashes of St. Joseph burning to the ground...

Flashes of his own church on fire...

The fire grew taller and burned brighter. From the glowing embers came a hand that reached out and touched his shoulder, giving him a newfound confidence that he thought he had lost.

"I understand."

"You understand what?" a voice asked.

CHAPTER
THIRTY·THREE

James opened his eyes and saw Branson at his bedside, his large hand on his shoulder.

"How long was I out?"

Branson smiled at him. "It's Saturday afternoon. About thirty-six hours since they admitted you. You remember anything?"

James closed his eyes. It had been almost two days since he had been admitted to the hospital, but he couldn't remember how he got there in the first place. He couldn't even recall what injury or illness he was suffering from. He remembered Simon, and the threat he posed, but not much else. He tried to sit up and a sharp pain radiated from his stomach.

"Whoa there, James. You were stabbed. You really don't remember anything, do you?"

"No. What happened to me?"

"Amy's ex stabbed you in the gut. Lucky though, nothing important got hit."

James looked down and saw bandages around his abdomen. There was a thick, syrupy smell of disinfectant. His hands and arms were also bandaged and sore.

"They stitched you up, but they had to put you out." Branson looked around to make sure no one overheard him. "They said you were spouting off about the devil being among us. Delusional, they said." Branson didn't look as though he thought James was delusional. He looked scared.

A sudden coldness washed through his body. He remembered Simon. He must have had something to do with this.

"Why can't I remember what happened to me?" James could see why he couldn't remember the surgery. They had sedated him. But why couldn't he remember anything about his injuries?

"Well, that's the thing. They ran a toxicology screening on you to check for drugs. You tested positive."

He had a bad feeling about this.

"Positive? Positive for what?" He didn't have to ask who drugged him.

"Scopolamine." Branson looked down before continuing. "On the streets it's called Devil's Breath."

"Devil's Breath? You're joking right?"

"Nope, they said you got a pretty good dose of it too."

"But how?"

"It's hard to say. The doctor said it's usually in powder form, odorless, tasteless. Could have been in the air, or in your food. It's used to take away people's free will. Makes you like a zombie."

"Could someone use this drug to make people do things they wouldn't normally do?"

"Yes. The doctor said people exposed to the drug become submissive. They appear fine, but their minds are highly susceptible to suggestion. The victim does whatever they're told. Criminals in some South American countries use it to get access to victims' bank accounts." Branson looked him in the eye. "It also causes amnesia and in some rare cases hallucinations."

All the strange behaviors his parishioners had displayed lately were starting to make sense. James had assumed that Simon was using some sort of otherworldly power to trick people. But it seemed possible that he was just drugging them.

Now James had been a victim of Simon's foul deeds himself. Try as he might, he could not remember anything. He had never experienced amnesia before, and he didn't like it at all.

"Daniel tested positive for it, and Rick too. The police say they've seen a couple of cases here over the past few weeks. People waking up in the park and not remembering how they got there. They've got their hands full with this flu, but the drugging is also a big concern.

I heard one doctor joke about this being the end of the world." Branson clearly had not seen the humor in that. Neither did James.

"Amy. How is Amy?" The chill in his belly deepened when the image of her smiling face appeared in his mind. He didn't know what he would do if something had happened to her while he slept.

"That girl cares about you. She was worried when you rushed off to Rick's the way you did. Called my church when she couldn't get a hold of you."

"She's okay?"

"Well, she's still sick with the flu. But Georgette is taking good care of her."

"Branson, I'm worried about Amy, and the rest of the people in Harmony. I think Simon has something to do with making people sick—or keeping them sick."

"That's just the scopolamine talking, son. It takes days to leave your system. You just need to worry about yourself getting back on your feet."

But James did think so. If he wasn't using scopolamine, then he was using something else. He just couldn't remember what it was. His mind raced with the possibilities. Finding the proof would have to wait, though. The doctor came in and told him he would have to spend one more night in the hospital for observation. He tried to rest and gather his strength for the battle that was sure to come.

CHAPTER
THIRTY - FOUR

The next morning, the nurse helped James out of the wheelchair and into Branson's car.

"You mind dropping me off at my car?"

"I already got your car for you. It's at the church. Where you too should be."

It was Sunday, and James wanted nothing more than to reunite with his flock. Things had been so out of the ordinary lately that he could use a bit of fellowship. He also wanted to check on the people who were sick.

"Good. I need to see if Simon's made anyone else sick while I was out."

"I understand your anguish over this, James," Branson said as he drove James to his church. "This is a nasty bug. I have some parishioners sick at home, too. Even got a few in the hospital. But what makes you think Simon—"

"Look, Branson," James interrupted, "I know this sounds crazy, but I told you about that town in Florida that got wiped out by a mysterious plague. I showed you the old newspaper clipping of Simon...and told you about the photo with Samuel in his youth. I know he has something to do with this illness too."

"Sometimes bad things happen, James. This is the world we live in. Diseases exist. People get sick. People get overwhelmed by their problems and turn to drugs."

"I know that. But I'm telling you what I know. Simon is going around to people's houses under false pretenses and after he leaves them they get sick. I don't think that's a coincidence."

The strange medicine he had unintentionally bought for Amy... That was it! The bottle in his car. That's what he was trying to remember. It had to be how Simon was making people sick.

Branson glanced at James for a moment and his grip on the steering wheel tightened. "Listen, James, the thought of this Simon guy walking up to my door or the door of someone I care about scares me too. But—"

"Branson, I have proof."

"What kind of proof?"

"The medicine! It has to be in the medicine."

"Medicine?" Branson asked.

James could tell from the man's expression that he needed to tread lightly here. Part of Branson had to be wondering if the scopolamine was still working its magic.

It sounded crazy, but he was certain that he was right.

"Yes, S'Wellness brand medicine. You ever heard of it?"

Branson shook his head.

"It's orange, smells foul, and has some sort of green slime swirling inside," James continued. "It almost looks alive. I have a bottle in my car. I'll show when we get to the church."

"That does sound strange," Branson's brow furrowed.

"I'm telling you, there is something wrong with this medicine, Branson. Caused by the devil or not, I'm sure it's got something to do with what's going on in Harmony right now."

Branson looked thoughtful for a moment as he pulled the car into the New Hope Church parking lot. The lot was at near capacity—which meant a packed house. Branson found a spot on the side of the church.

"Let me make a phone call."

"You've got an idea?" James asked, unsure of how they would get someone else to believe them. But was willing to do whatever it took to get to the bottom of this. Even if it made him seem like he had lost his mind.

"Not an idea, a friend. He lives in New York. He's sort of a disease detective."

James nodded. "I'll grab the bottle out of my—" He paused.

Behind the church a shadowy figure lurked. Someone dressed in dark clothing was pouring something on the ground.

"What's he doing?"

"Watering the garden?" Branson suggested. He didn't sound convinced.

"That's no watering can. That's…that's a gasoline can. He's going to burn down the church!"

CHAPTER
THIRTY-FIUE

"**C**all 9-1-1 and get everyone out," James said, exiting the car, "I'm going to stop to him!"

"God help you," Branson said as they parted ways.

James raced to the back of the church shouting, "Stop! Stop!"

The man dressed in the black hooded sweatshirt continued to splash the contents of a gasoline can onto the ground. He wasn't even paying attention to what was going on around him.

"You can't do this! This is a sacred place," James shouted at the macabre figure.

With his back to James the man stood straight up, holding the can dripping at his side. Lifting the can, he doused the rest of the container over himself, soaking the baggy sweatshirt that hid his true identity.

"Don't! This is wrong. You have to know that," James said, trying to appeal to his sense of right and wrong, but there didn't seem to be anything that he could do to prevent what was about to happen. "This must be hard for you to realize, but the devil is controlling your actions. On some level, you must be able to feel it. This isn't right. You know it isn't."

The man dropped the can, knocking it on its side, dribbling the remaining liquid onto the ground. It pooled underneath James' feet. The gasoline vapors seared his nostrils.

"He uses a powerful drug to control your actions," James continued. "He has been doing this all over town. He uses our past transgressions against us." James took another step closer. "God does not hold past transgressions against us. He understands our failings. The only way to thwart this evil man is for you to confess your sins."

The man pulled a gold lighter from his pant pocket. James stood his ground.

"The devil can be beaten with the truth and God on your side."

The man flicked the lighter.

Nothing happened.

"Whatever your sin is, it can't be as bad as what you are doing right now."

He flicked the lighter again.

Again, nothing.

"Open your eyes and see that what you are doing here

is wrong. You're allowing the devil to have a hold on you. Show your face and let me help you."

Finally the man in the cloak of gasoline turned and faced James for the first time.

His eyes were hidden in the dankness of the hood that billowed around and darkened his face. His head was tilted down, and he was either unable or unwilling to lift it to reveal his face. It had to be somebody that had been tainted by Simon's influence.

"The only way to win against the devil is to beat him at his own game. Stop hiding in the shadows and walk into the light. Use my voice as your guide. Everything will be okay."

A weak, strained voice came from the hooded man. "No. Not okay. It's so dark out."

James couldn't place the voice, but the words... There was something familiar about them.

"There's an evil in our town, Reverend!"

James' heart raced as he stepped closer, grabbed the top of the hood, and pulled it off. For the first time he was at a loss for words. He stepped back from the man that he thought he knew.

"I have to...do this Reverend."

The pitiful voice was coming out of the parched lips of Samuel Stirling.

CHAPTER
THIRTY - SIX

After Branson managed to get the ushers to assist in getting the church evacuated and called 9-1-1, he ran back to James' side.

"Samuel, you've atoned for your sins a long time ago," said James in a reassuring voice. "You've been a good Christian and have never strayed from the word of God since." James was sure of Samuel's belief in the Holy Spirit and the strength of faith. There had to be a way to get through to him.

Branson, on the other hand, saw something sinister and dark at work in Samuel's face. In Samuel's eyes he saw doubt and misgivings—here was a man who needed convincing. "Samuel," Branson said, "I know we haven't known each other for very long, but I see a man of unshakable faith inside you. He wants to do the right thing. Deep down, you are more than a good person—you are a child of God. Whatever it is that's troubling you, you have to voice it and surrender yourself to Him and His goodness. If you don't, it will fester inside of you. It will allow the devil's will to take root and grow there. Don't let him do this to you, Samuel. To all of these innocent people!"

Samuel took a deep breath and cast his eyes towards James. They looked strange, as if the clear blue of his eyes had been replaced with a swirling blackness. The blackness receded briefly but then surged again. A battle was being waged inside the frail old man, and it appeared that the darkness was winning.

"I...I...don't know where to begin. All of this seems like a bad dream. The things that I have seen myself do will haunt me for the rest of my life." He paused and looked back and forth between the two men of God. The evil in his eyes expanded once more. "This church must be destroyed...Must be destroyed."

He was fighting his demons, and losing with every second that passed.

"Samuel, I need you to tell us what it is," James pleaded.

"I...don't know if I can...been holding on to this... must destroy the...Noooo!"

Samuel put his head down, shoulders shaking with effort, and panted like a man who had just won a race. He raised his eyes, and the piercing blue of his color of his irises had returned. He had won. He looked sad, and scared, but the evil influence had passed.

James could see that letting out this secret was the only way in which Samuel could come to terms with what he had done.

"My friend…Pastor Griffin…I killed my friend. He saved me and I killed him…this is my confession. May God have mercy on me!" Samuel sank to his knees and started to cry.

"Pastor Griffin? No, Samuel, he's not dead. He moved away. To Florida." James glanced at Branson. "Right?"

Branson didn't look well. His lips had gone gray and a cold sweat broke out on his forehead. "I thought so, but it did seem odd the way he just left a note and didn't say goodbye to anyone in person. The parishioners were sorely disappointed. No one's heard a word from him since he left."

Sirens sounded in the distance.

Branson and James looked at Samuel expectantly.

"I killed him with my own bare hands. I could see everything that I was doing, but…" Samuel looked down at his own hands. "I had no control over my own body."

Even now, Samuel's hands were struggling to stay under his own command. "I buried him in the garden. He loved his garden." Samuel's hand was visibly shaking. The lighter he had been holding dropped to the ground and his shoulders slumped. "Why Reverend? Why did I do it?"

"This is the devil's doing, Samuel. It's time for you to break free of his power."

James watched as Samuel broke down, sobbing. "Please help me, Reverend," he cried.

James knelt down, took Samuel's hand and prayed, "O merciful Father, our only help in time of need, look in pity upon Samuel, Your servant, who is troubled. Give him some token of Your forgiveness. Fill his heart with joy and peace. Keep him ever in Your love and obedience. Let him live to bring forth some good fruit, which shall assure him of Your pardon. Grant this, O Lord, for the sake of Jesus Christ, our Savior. Amen."

Samuel looked up at James with hope in his eyes.

"God loves you Samuel. We'll get you the help you need."

He hoped it would be enough.

CHAPTER
THIRTY - SEVEN

Fifteen minutes later James and Branson left Samuel in the capable hands of the paramedics. In between sobs, he whispered about the garden, asking James and Branson to 'find the body.' James offered to ride with him to the hospital, but Samuel refused. Said he was needed here.

"God wants you here, Reverend," he had said, as they wheeled him away.

Most of the people that had been inside the church had gone home and the grounds were beginning to fill with firemen and police officers. James and Branson needed to find out what they could before they were asked to leave.

"Over here!" Branson called. He was standing under a willow tree, next to what appeared to be a slight mound.

James swallowed thickly and tried to clear his throat. He had no words. He just walked over to the gently swaying tree. Beneath the low-hanging branches was a shallow grave. It looked recently disturbed, as though animals, or possibly Samuel, had tried to unearth the body that lay within.

The two horrified men saw a torso and an arm, but the rest was buried in the loose dirt. Branson took a deep breath and looked heavenward.

The body was unrecognizable. It appeared to be a man, but James couldn't even be sure of that much. He had expected the corpse to smell, but the only scent in the air was musty dirt and a hint of aster blossoms. As he silently prayed, James crouched down and gently brushed the dirt off of a dark blue windbreaker. "Do you recognize this jacket?"

Branson glanced down and nodded solemnly, tears springing to his eyes. Distasteful as it was, James reached into the jacket, trying to find something that could help them positively identify the body. He had to keep looking, even though both men knew who the victim was likely to be. There was a solid bulge in the inner breast pocket. James pulled out a dusty wallet.

"James! We should leave that for the police." Branson looked aghast.

"We need to find out for sure who this is."

In spite of his objections, Branson made no move to stop James from continuing to search the wallet.

James brushed the dirt off the wallet and let it fall open. There was a clear pocket that held a state-issued ID card. The name and picture were that of Charles Griffin.

"Well?" Branson asked.

"It's him." James said, thumbing through the business cards and photos inside the small billfold, desperate for another clue.

His heart stopped when he saw it.

Inside the pastor's wallet was a business card for S'Wellness Pharmaceuticals. There was no name, no address, just the S'Wellness logo.

James flashed the card to Branson. "This can't be a coincidence." He flipped the card over. "There's something written on the back. Something about a job. Did Pastor Griffin have another job?"

"Well, no, I can't say that he did. Let me take a look at it." Branson reached for the card with a trembling hand. "It's his writing, I'm fairly certain." He squinted at the hastily scrawled note.

"Something about a job on February seventh?" James asked. "Or was he meeting someone at 2:17 p.m.?"

Branson's eyes lit up. "Nope. That's not a date, not a time. It's a clue. It says Job 2:7. '*So Satan went out from the presence of the Lord and afflicted Job with painful sores from the soles of his feet to the crown of his head*.'"

The breath left James' body. "Give it here. I'm putting it back." He snatched the wallet from Branson.

"Wait!" Branson said, grabbing James by the arm. At

that moment Officer Anthony Rodriguez and several Harmony police officers rounded the corner of the building.

James waved them over and handed Officer Rodriguez the wallet. "We found this on the body. It's Pastor Griffin."

Officer Rodriguez grabbed the wallet from James with a gloved hand and placed it into an evidence bag. Visibly upset, the officer asked, "You disturbed the body?"

"We were just trying to help," James said.

"Reverend, you intentions may have been good, but as a result, you've inadvertently contaminated the crime scene. You've left behind fingerprints, footprints, and possibly even DNA evidence. Now, I need to account for that evidence."

"We found this too," Branson said, handing Officer Rodriguez the S'Wellness business card he had been holding. "We think it may have something to do with his death."

"Leave the detective work to the professionals, Reverend. Barnes, get them out of my crime scene."

After a brief interview with Officer Barnes, James and Branson were led outside of the yellow tape that surrounded the church, where they lingered in silence.

The garden bustled with activity as the authorities started the delicate work of documenting the scene and exhuming the body.

The eerie silence was interrupted by a frantic voice.

"Reverend Buchman! Reverend Buchman!"

It was Georgette Newman.

"Georgette, what is it? Is everything okay?"

"Tried calling you," she said, trying to catch her breath.

James glanced at his phone. No signal.

"James, it's Amy... She got worse...much worse. Had to call 9-1-1... They took her to the hospital!"

A panic that James had only experienced once before flooded his body. He looked to Branson.

"Go!" his friend said. "I'll have my guy look into S'Wellness and meet up with you later."

Seconds later James was in his car and speeding back to the same hospital he'd just been released from a couple hours earlier.

CHAPTER THIRTY-EIGHT

James rushed out of the hospital elevator onto the third floor and into the Intensive Care Unit. The sounds of suffering—people crying, coughing, and whispering in low tones, reverberated through the halls.

He passed a small chapel on his way to the nurse's station. The chapel, at least, looked like a welcoming and warm space. He made a mental note to remember it in case he needed a quiet place to talk with God.

There were two women working at the ICU nurse's station. The larger of the two, who wore a colorful smock that had little ducks carrying umbrellas printed all over it, looked up at him with tired brown eyes and a slight scowl. "Can I help you?" she asked.

"My name is Pastor James Buchman. I'm here to see Amy Sheridan."

"Are you family?"

"No. I'm…I'm…"

"Her pastor?" the other nurse finished for him.

"Yes."

"It's all right, Carla, I've got this." She turned to James. "I'm Briella."

The petite nurse waved for him to follow her. He nodded at Carla, who was still scowling at him like she had caught him cheating on a test.

"She doesn't like to be interrupted, does she?" James asked as he followed along behind his guide, whose ashy blonde hair was coming loose from her haphazard bun.

Briella shrugged. "She's been working double shifts. We all have." She stopped in front of room 307 and poked her head in the door before turning to look back at James. "I'm glad you came to sit with Amy, Reverend. The only thing we can do for her now is to make her comfortable. She needs someone to be with her. You need anything, you give me a call, you hear?"

A voice sounded from the intercom, summoning anyone who was available to come to the Emergency Room. She did her best to smile warmly at him before she walked away, but James could see the fatigue etched into her face.

"Bless you, Briella," he called after her.

The door to the room was open and James went in to find Amy, hooked up to two different IV bags. Lead wires from a monitoring machine were attached to her chest and arms. She opened her eyes and saw James as he sat down in a chair next to the bed. "James?"

"I'm here Amy. I'm right here," he said, trying not to wince at the obvious pain in her voice. "You okay?"

Amy nodded her head, though the effort appeared to pain her. Her usual porcelain complexion had gone gray and her lips were cracked and dry from breathing through her mouth. "Why do you smell like gasoline?" she asked, a thin smile stretching her lips.

If she knew why he smelled like gas, she wouldn't be smiling. He forced himself to smile back at her and tried to think of a witty reply. Whenever he was around Amy, even now when she was so sick, he found himself fumbling for words.

"Your hands!" Amy's eyes grew wider as she took in his appearance, including the stiff bandages on his forearms.

James was grateful that she couldn't see the bandages below his shirt, and his stab wound throbbed in response to his thoughts. He grimaced. "I'll be okay. Maybe a few scars." He didn't want to worry her, not when she was so weak.

"Did Rick—?" she said, with a wheeze. "I'm so sorry James." She coughed softly and her eyes squinted closed for a moment.

James shook his head. "It wasn't your fault."

"He's…damaged," she admitted. "I knew that before I started going out with him. I thought I could help. But once I was with him, I found out he didn't really want any help."

James nodded. What could he say? Rick had been trouble before Amy stated dating him. But that wasn't the only factor at play. Simon had preyed on that cracked psyche to achieve his own ends.

"I shouldn't have gotten you involved." Her voice cracked, and James worried she might begin to cry.

"No, you did the right thing Amy. Rick could have hurt you very badly. I never would have forgiven myself had I allowed that to happen."

She looked up at him from the pale blue bed with sparkling eyes full of tears and admiration. "You're a good man James Buchman."

James put his hand over Amy's own. Her hand was thin, and her skin dry.

A single fat tear rolled down her pale cheek. "I don't want to die James."

He wouldn't allow himself to think that she wasn't going to make it. "Amy, I'm sure that God has a lot more that He wants you to do here before you join Him." He met her gaze. She closed her eyes and a few more slow tears slipped free. James looked away. He didn't want her to see the look on his face. He was sure it was full of panic and sorrow despite his best efforts to stay cheerful and calm.

Amy didn't speak again for a while. He wasn't sure if she had fallen asleep or was just resting. Or...

"Can I get you some water, Amy?" James asked. His heart ached.

"Hmm..." She cleared her throat. She looked as if she was in a lot of pain, but she was still alive. It seemed so unfair that they had just started getting to know one another and now he might be losing her. He tried to shake the feeling of dread that had haunted him since she became so ill.

Amy smacked her lips and said, "No. No water, thanks. Hurts to swallow. I wish I wasn't...wasn't sick. I wish we could spend more time together. But if now is my time, then I guess I'm ready."

Was it really Amy's time? If this sickness that plagued Harmony was unnatural—if it was something that Satan himself had actually brought here to infect people, then was it really Amy's time? She was so young and had a long life ahead of her. Could Simon's evildoing be God's plan for the smart, beautiful young woman? Could it be His plan for the entire town of people, James' people? Even though he had not been in Harmony long, they were just that—his people.

God's will or not, it was obvious that Amy wasn't getting any better, nor were the countless other citizens he could hear suffering in the packed hospital. Nurses and doctors were being paged over the intercom. He could hear them running past Amy's open door. He had to do something to help, but what could he do?

Emotion thickened his voice as he asked, "Amy,

would it be all right if I prayed with you?"

Amy smiled that same weak smile. "I'd like that."

He clasped Amy's hand within both of his own, and then James bowed his head and closed his eyes.

"O heavenly Father, we humbly beseech You, look upon Amy, Your sick servant, and relieve her pain. Grant her the sweet sense of Your presence. Let her not doubt Your goodness or love in her illness, but wait in patience until Your correction has produced in her, Your perfect work. Bless all that is done for her recovery that will be according to Your wisdom. Comfort her by the loving ministration of those who care for her, and in Your good time, restore her again to her usual heath, humbled and taught by this affliction. And this we ask for Jesus' sake. Amen"

When James looked up again, Amy's eyes were closed and she was breathing peacefully. Her chest moved up and down beneath the drab blue hospital sheets. James wiped the tears from his own eyes and glanced at the heart monitor's display. Amy's heartbeat was weak, but steady. If Amy was going to die, it wasn't going to be right now.

And then an alarm sounded.

There was a flurry of activity out in the hallway as both nurses ran from their station past his door. A voice came from the loudspeaker, "Code blue, room three-oh-four. Code blue, room three-oh-four." Although James was a man of God and not a doctor, even he knew that code blue was hospital-speak for when someone's heart had stopped and they needed immediate resuscitation.

He stepped out into the hallway in time to see a doctor with a grim look on his face rushing down the hall and another worker in scrubs wheeling in a cart with several drawers through the door of room 304. Shouting and hurried orders spilled from inside the room. The snap and hiss of defibrillator paddles being applied to a patient's chest echoed in the hallway. The rest of the floor had grown eerily quiet. It was as if the whole world was waiting on the outcome of the heroic efforts of the hospital staff.

The results of their efforts became obvious as the nurse who had led him to Amy's room, Briella, came out and leaned against the wall wiping tears from her eyes. She looked up and met James' eyes.

"Oh. Sorry, Reverend. I didn't realize you were..." She trailed off, looking back into that room. "That's the third one we've lost today. This...sickness... Whatever it is, is killing people." Briella wiped at her eyes as she walked quickly past him to answer a ringing phone. How many hours she had been working without a break, with people dying all around her?

Suddenly, James had a strong urge to find out who had died in room 304. Without thinking he walked lightly to the room, his shoes making no sound against the tile floor. At the door, he peered in and saw a small crowd still gathered around the hospital bed. One person stood out. He wasn't wearing scrubs or a mask. It was Philip Falcone, leaning over the bed rail, sobbing.

James glanced past Philip. The woman in the bed was Philip's wife, Melissa. James backed out of the doorway and into the hall. He pressed his back against the wall and slid down until he was squatting. He covered his eyes with his hands but the tears just didn't come. He was in shock and couldn't move, as if his feet were frozen in place.

CHAPTER
THIRTY - NINE

A wave of hopelessness overcame James, and something in him woke up. He wouldn't go down without a fight. He wasn't going to let Simon take the lives of these innocent people, not while he was still breathing. Adrenaline surged in his blood and he put one foot in front of the other. Nothing would be resolved if he didn't get moving down the busy hallway.

James looked at the various rooms and curtained-off sections that the staff had set up when they'd run out of rooms. A strong force pulled him toward the doors of rooms that housed patients he had never even met. His heart told him to go to each of the sick and sit with them and pray. He didn't know where it came from, this assurance of what he needed to do, but it was right.

The first room he ducked into was dim, but the patient

seemed to be awake and aware of his surroundings. James showed the middle-aged man the book he carried. The man saw it, nodded, and held out his calloused hand. James took it firmly in his own and the man let out a wheezing sigh. James was both honored and relieved that he was allowed to share this man's life with him when he was suffering so badly.

"What is your name?" he asked the ailing patient.

"Willie, Willie Bowlish," he whispered, with some effort. His eyes closed, and James took that for his cue to get started.

James flipped through his prayer book until he found the words he needed to ease the man's suffering. He found a suitable passage that somehow felt right.

"O Lord and heavenly Father, we come before You with humble thanks for all your mercies, more especially for the means of grace which You have afforded Willie, in this interruption to his usual course of health. We thank You for reminding him that his enjoyment of the blessings of this world will not last forever—that things in which he commonly takes delight will one day come to cease to please him. Lord, deliver Willie from all impatience and all fear from his body, and fill him at the same time with spiritual fear—let him not be afraid of pain or sickness, but let him be afraid of You, and not waste the opportunity which You are affording him. Restore him in Your good time to his usual health, and grant that this interruption may purify his soul's health, making it not an evil to him, but an infinite blessing, for the sake of Jesus Christ our Savior. Amen."

The dim room appeared to have brightened when James looked up, and Willie was smiling up at him from the bed.

"Amen. Thank you. Thank you," the man managed to mutter before drifting off into what appeared to be a peaceful sleep. His breathing had evened out as they were praying, and now he was hardly wheezing at all.

James held his hand in silence for a few more minutes. Reality seemed richer now, and he wasn't sure if it was adrenaline or the fog of Simon's treachery lifting from his soul. Either way, he had a plan now. He had found at least one way to fight back against him, devil or not. James had the weapons of faith and prayer to fight with.

He gently rested Willie's hand at his side, careful not to wake him. The monitors beeped reassuringly as James left the room.

Even the hallway seemed less desperate now that James was driven by purpose, and he strode into the next room, and the next, repeating his prayers and pleas for salvation. Each time, he was certain that he saw the patients improving when he opened his eyes after saying Amen.

The staff got to go home as another shift began, and new nurses and doctors started showing up to check on the stricken patients. James smiled broadly at them, trying to impart some grace and reassurance. The hospital seemed quieter, and less dark, even though evening was well upon them by now.

CHAPTER FORTY

James had lost track of time hours ago, but he had visited and prayed with more than ten patients. Some were strangers to him, like Willie had been, while others he knew from his congregation. Mindy Ellison and Emily Watson were both resting calmly now after his visit to their respective rooms. George Alvarez was also ailing in one of the makeshift, curtained-off areas. James had prayed with him and left him in better spirits.

George had lifted James' spirit as well. Just before James left his room, George called out to him. "Pastor! I think just being near a person that is so close to God has shown me that my time on this earth is not up yet. Thank you for sharing your gift with me." The tears in his eyes had been of the happy variety.

Other patients said similar things to him after they prayed together, and each time James gave thanks to God that His plan seemed to be working. He was easing the suffering of the stricken, even of a few patients who were in the hospital for other ailments. James hoped the power of prayer could help prevent Simon's wickedness from touching them in the first place.

More than once, he had poked his head into Amy's room. She was sleeping, and it looked like a restful sleep, so he didn't wake her. She looked so peaceful that it strengthened him to see her suffering so vastly reduced. He hoped her dreams were kind to her.

A few patients had refused to pray with him, and one had even shrunk away from his touch. He wasn't sure if it was him or his religion they objected to, or if they were just delusional and frightened. He did his best to respect their wishes, praying silently by their doors even though he was fairly certain it wouldn't be enough.

And sure enough, it wasn't. One of the patients who had refused his offer of prayer died shortly after turning him down, as the medical team had been unable to resuscitate him.

The loss was a painful blow to James, but he had to keep working until he had touched the hands and souls of every patient in the hospital. He tried not to let the death affect his energy, and strode purposefully into the next room.

Inside, Officer John Colmenero stood over his wife,

Nancy. He wore his police uniform, as though he had been called away from his shift to be at his wife's side. She wasn't moving, and her skin was pale and damp. James extended a hand to John, whose handshake was firm despite his desperate situation.

"She's dying," John said mournfully. "She hasn't woken for hours, and her breathing…"

"We mustn't give up hope, John," James said, with what he hoped was a good mixture of calmness and confidence. He fingered the well-worn pages of his prayer journal, looking for a certain passage. He knew it by heart, but he liked to see the words on the page, written in his father's bold hand. He placed the open book on the bed so that, in a way, his father could be present, at least in James' heart.

He walked to the other side of the bed, took Nancy's hand and extended his other hand to John across her prone body. John took James' hand, and gently picked up his wife's other hand. The men bowed their heads, and James felt stronger and more connected than he had all night. The three formed a circle of faith that energized and invigorated him.

"God of all comfort, we come to You for the assurance of Your presence and blessing. We thank You that Christ has assured us that our life is precious. Look graciously upon Nancy, Your servant. Let her rest in sense of Your love and goodness. Bless the means by which are used for her cure. Give skills to the physicians, and compassion to all of them that shall assist in the work. Restore her quickly so that she may go into Your house, and praise Your name for Your wonderful goodness, in Jesus Christ our Lord. Amen."

He had not needed to look at the book to recite the familiar words, and he was filled with a glowing feeling that grew in intensity as he had delivered the message to John and his wife.

John echoed, "Amen."

From her sickbed, Nancy murmured, "Amen." Her face was beaded with sweat from her fever breaking, but she looked more alert. Her eyes were open, and there was even a hint of a smile at the edge of her mouth.

Something shifted. The weight upon his shoulders that had been steadily growing since Simon came to town was beginning to lighten. The hospital itself appeared less gloomy, the patients and staff alike seemed energized and more alive. There hadn't been a death in hours, and there was even a tinkling laugh of a nurse in the hall.

The laughter was welcome after the stresses of the day, and James finally felt that he might be able to take a break. There were a few rooms he had yet to visit, but even those patients he hadn't seen were improving. It was as if the air itself had grown more pure, and all the pain was being replaced with hope and courage.

John was shedding silent tears and stroking his wife's hair. His joy at her improvement warmed James, and he moved to leave the room so that they could be alone. He passed by a chair where Nancy's purse sat open with its contents in full view and froze in his tracks.

In the purse was a bottle of S'Wellness brand medicine.

"John...where did you get this?" He tried to keep his rising panic away from his voice. Seeing the bottle had shaken him right when he was feeling so positive about the results of his work. He saw Simon's face in the swirling green, but when he blinked, it was gone.

"Oh that? Philip Falcone gave it to us. Why?"

"Did you give this to Nancy? When did she last have a dose?"

"Yeah, she was taking it at home, but didn't seem to help at all. I can't remember the last time she took it," he said, sounding confused. "I can't remember. How 'bout that?"

James steeled himself against the revulsion that bubbled within and grabbed the bottle. He threw it in the trash and tied up the otherwise empty bag that lined the bin. He took the bag with him, and said, "You won't be needing this anymore."

In the hall, he finally looked at the clock and saw that it was nearly five, Monday morning. He had prayed with everyone in the ICU and all the other patients on the floor they had set up as a makeshift quarantine for the flu. There was only one more thing he needed to do before he could go home to get some rest.

The door to Amy's room was still ajar, and she was

still fast asleep. He pulled a chair up to her bedside and bowed his head. He thanked God for showing him the way, and for the opportunity to share the strength of his faith with His other children.

PART FOUR

and that they will come to their senses and
escape from the trap of the devil, who has taken
them captive to do his will.

– 2 Timothy 2:26 (NIV)

CHAPTER
FORTY-ONE

James didn't realize he had fallen asleep until late that morning when Georgette arrived to take over the vigil at Amy's bedside. She pressed a cool hand to his forehead to wake him. He had fallen asleep in a chair in Amy's hospital room. An uncomfortable chair, he noticed as he sat up, yawning and stretching. His head was swirling with the remnants of dreams and thoughts of a new tactic to deal with Simon's machinations.

"Good morning," said a familiar voice.

He looked up to see Amy smiling at him over a tray of breakfast. The smell of coffee and eggs helped bring him fully to his senses. "Good morning," James said, patting all his pockets, looking for his phone. "What time is it? Why didn't you wake me?"

"Almost eleven o'clock. You looked so peaceful

sleeping there," she said over a bite of toast. "Want some coffee?"

Georgette was positively beaming. "Look at her, reverend. She's eating."

"And hospital food too," James said. "She must really be feeling better."

She certainly looked better. There was still a slight grayish cast to her skin, but Amy's eyes were bright and her voice was stronger. He gave silent thanks to God.

James painfully unfolded himself from the hospital lounge chair, wincing as each cut and bruise on his body made itself known.

"You need to rest," protested Georgette.

"I'm fine," James said, and that was partially true. Seeing the improvement in Amy's condition gave him strength… and a burning curiosity to check on the other people he had prayed with on the ward last night.

"At least eat something," Amy said. "I'm never going to finish all of this." She pushed the bedside tray toward him.

James glanced at the half eaten scrambled eggs on her plate and his mouth watered. He must be starving to salivate over hospital food. "Are you sure?" he asked.

"Positive," Amy smiled. "And have this," she said, holding out a sealed cup of apple juice. "I've never been a fan."

"Thank you," he said and eased back down into the chair, balancing the plate and cup of juice on his knees.

He downed the slightly rubbery, but still edible eggs in three bites, and washed it down with the juice.

The doctor he had seen looking so flustered the day before entered Amy's room. He was clearly tired, but looked much more at ease. James stood, feeling slightly guilty about eating Amy's food.

The doctor smiled wearily at him. "I can ask the nurse to bring you one of your own," he offered.

"Thank you, but I'm good."

"You truly are," the doctor agreed. "You brought a sense of peace to the ward last night. The patients rested easier after your visits, and their fevers broke, each and every one of them. If I were a believer I'd say it was a miracle…"

"You can say it even if you're not," said Georgette.

"I believe in the power of science," said the doctor. "And the power of the human mind."

"Those powers come from God," James told him. "They are His gifts."

Amy smiled. "It looks like you are a believer after all, doctor."

"Maybe I am, then," he said. "And right now, I'd like to use the power of medical science to give you a short exam to see just how much better you are this morning."

James took that as his cue and stood to make an exit, remembering to pick up the trash bag containing the bottle of noxious S'Wellness fluid.

Georgette and Amy exchanged puzzled looks.

"You ladies will have to excuse me. Georgette, you'll keep an eye on Amy, right?"

"Oh sure, I'm happy to!" She did look like she was in her element as she fluttered around the room opening the curtains and tidying up the already tidy space.

"Amy…" He looked at her and was suddenly overwhelmed. It was not just her he was trying to protect, but she represented the good people he was charged with caring for. He quickly turned his eyes away. "I'll be back in to see you later, okay?"

"Maybe you could bring me a cheeseburger?"

James looked at her and then at the doctor.

"Maybe," the doctor said.

Out in the corridor, James could truly feel the sense of peace the doctor had mentioned. Without a doubt that it was the love of God. Medicine might help, but the minds that create it would be guided by God's hand. The power to fight this evil disease was bound within the pages of the Good Book. The power of God's Word carried within fueled James.

CHAPTER FORTY-TWO

As James breezed past the nurse's station, a nurse he hadn't seen yet poked her head out over the counter.

"Pastor Buchman?"

"Yes?" He looked at her again closely, but didn't recognize her.

"You're the one who stayed up all night with the patients, right?"

"I am."

"I'd like to show you something." She stood and motioned for him to follow her to one of the rooms. They stood in the open doorway and peered in.

It took James a moment to recognize the person he saw in the first room. It was Willie Bowlish, the first man he had prayed with the day before, and he looked like a completely different person. He was eating as well, and was sitting up. He smiled and waved when he saw James in the doorway. James waved back, with his heart in his throat. The nurse took him into the hall.

"Can you believe this? He looked so bad yesterday, and today he's eating and drinking. He even walked a little bit. His fever broke, last night." She crooked her finger to beckon him.

They looked in the next door, and James saw another patient sitting up and looking alert. Her family was with her, and they were all smiling and happy. Faint laughter was coming from the room. Laughter where the night before there had been only misery. They continued through the hall, checking in on all the patients.

"Their fevers started breaking, all of them almost at once. They started getting better. It's a miracle we only lost one patient last night." She leaned in conspiratorially. "If we hadn't gotten this under control, I think they would have quarantined the whole town."

One death.

"What was that patient's name?" He asked.

One death. One too many.

"Patrick Chandler. He was pretty bad off when he got here. But then again, they were all looking pretty bad yesterday." Her smile faded and he could tell that she felt Patrick's death keenly, despite the positive results for the other patients. He patted her on the shoulder.

"I'm so glad to see that you nurses and doctors were

able to help everyone. We are all grateful for your efforts." He meant it with all his heart. He may have played a part in breaking whatever spell or disease Simon had unleashed here, but the folks at the hospital had handled the crisis like a well-oiled machine.

"It's our job," she said graciously. "Probably not much different from your job, I think."

"I shared the Word with them, yes. That's my job."

"Well, I think what you do is just as important as what we do." Tears sparkled in her eyes. A phone rang back at the nurse's station. "Duty calls. Bless you, pastor."

She couldn't know the impact her words had on James. Yesterday, he had been so near to giving up. He was helpless in the face of all the suffering.

With the light of the new day had come a change, a sense of peace, and a lessening of the burden shouldered by himself and his parishioners. He had God to thank for that.

Still, the loss of Patrick's life darkened his joy at the miraculous recovery of the patients. He wanted to save all of them. Had his prayer come too late? Had the man doomed himself by refusing to take James' hand in prayer? James preferred to believe the former, but he couldn't help but wonder if the healing power of the prayer would have been stronger had the man joined him.

James passed Patrick's empty room. They had stripped the sheets from the bed, and there was no evidence that anyone had ever been there. He said a silent prayer for the man's soul.

Before leaving the hospital, James paused in the tiny chapel and gave thanks to God.

When he was finished he took out his phone, but hesitated. "I hope You won't mind me using this in Your house, but I think we are going to need all the help we can get as soon as we can get it. I want to fill this entire town with the power of Your love."

With that, James called a few of the deacons of his church and asked them to go to anyone and everyone who was still sick and to pray with them, and to spread the word for all members of the congregation who were well to do the same.

He tried Branson, but there was no answer.

He had to reach him and tell him what had happened. His heart was full of hope, and it was a welcome feeling. There may be more battles yet to come, but he was armed with God's love and His Word, and he was that much stronger for it.

CHAPTER
FORTY · THREE

As James made his way to his car he held the trash bag away from his body. A chill emanated from the bottle of S'Wellness it contained. He opened the trunk of his car and tossed it inside and then closed the trunk lid to see the grinning face of Simon suddenly standing there, his fedora in his hand.

"Good morning, Reverend," Simon said in a cheery voice. "Fine day, isn't it?"

"Not if you've lost a loved one to this illness," James responded coldly.

Simon managed to make his eyes look sad even as the smile stayed firmly in place. "Yes. Poor people. But their loved ones are in a far better place now, don't you think? At least most of them..."

"What do you want Simon?"

"Just wanted to check on Amy and a few other friends," Simon said, pointing to the hospital.

James had the strongest desire to punch the man in his face. That would knock that smile loose. But he restrained himself. "I know you spent some time with Amy before she got sick. I know you went to see a lot of people before they got sick. Got sick and died, I mean. In fact, I wouldn't be surprised if everyone who is sick told me they remembered seeing you just before they got sick."

"Well now, that would make me one busy little bee, wouldn't it?" Simon leaned back against an SUV parked next to James' car and played with the brim of his hat. "It's too bad you can't help these poor sick people, isn't it, Reverend? Oh, you may have helped them through the night, and I see that you're feeling a bit smug about that, but what you did is temporary, I assure you. If only there was some way for you to do...something that will last. Something that would help permanently!"

"You seem to have something in mind. What are you suggesting, Simon?"

"A deal? Why, Reverend, are you asking to make a deal with me?"

"I don't deal with the devil," he said automatically. "I'm just wondering what your terms would be."

"Why, Reverend, I've already told you my terms. They are very simple. Just one in fact. Leave."

"That's it?"

"You've got it. Get out of town. Move. Go somewhere else. Relocate. Scram. Take a hike. Leave. Leave today. Leave now. Do that and I guarantee that all those people that are sick, including Amy, will get better, and stay that way."

"No," James said to him.

A shadow passed across Simon's face though the sky was clear. "You know, priest," Simon growled, his voice suddenly lower and rougher, "I don't understand why you cling to this bad habit of telling me no."

"Because I don't see it as a bad habit."

"Kind of bad in this case," Simon said. He gestured at the hospital behind him. "You really want those people to die? Do you? Because I can promise you they will die! They will all succumb to this illness and in less than a month's time this whole town will be a memory—a ghost town. A cautionary tale for people to behave or the devil will come sneaking in and murder them in their sleep. And now, because you refuse to leave, Amy is going to die too. She's going to die, priest! What're you going to do about that? Just stand there playing with your morals? She's going to die!"

"No she's not," James said quietly.

Simon stopped mid-rant, one arm in the air. "What?"

"She's not going to die. Neither are any of the people you made sick."

"There is nothing you can do to stop it."

"Yes, there is. We both know it's true. Amy was sicker

than several of the people who have died. The doctors didn't think she'd make it through the night, but she lived. Not only that, but everyone is getting better as we speak. Do you know why?"

Simon glared at him but didn't respond.

"Well, I'll tell you why," James went on. "They all prayed with me. It's that simple. The only difference between those poor people who died and those that lived is that they gave the problem over to God through prayer. And they're going to live."

For the first time since finding out who Simon was, who he *really* was, James stood up to the man and looked him squarely in the eyes. "So here's what I'm going to do. I'm going to make my rounds, and pray with as many of these poor souls as I can—the ones that you've poisoned and tried to kill—and I'm going to help God save most of them."

"Not all of them priest," Simon told him with smiling contempt.

James shrugged. "No. Not all of them. I wish I could, but some of them can't or won't be reached. The thing you're forgetting is I'm not alone anymore. I'm not the only one who knows what you are. Not the only one who's standing up against you."

The devil stared, mouth hanging open, and then broke into a loud laugh, clutching his sides for laughing so hard. "You really are something else. I tell you what, little man, I tell you what. You leave now, and we'll call it square. Nobody else has to get sick if you leave right now. On the other hand," he stopped laughing and put the tip of his finger right in James' face, "if you don't leave, right here, right now, all bets are off. You can save as many as you like, by staying and praying your little prayers. But people will still get sick. You can't stop that."

"Maybe he can't," Branson said, walking up behind them, "but I have a friend who can. Mornin', James." He stepped up and turned to Simon. "Mr. Paradis, isn't it? I don't think we've been formally introduced."

Simon ignored Branson's outstretched hand. "Ah, the other priest. So, you're going to stop me, are you?"

Branson shook his head. "Yes, but not just me. I have friends. One friend is a man who works at the Centers for Disease Control and Prevention. Good to have contacts, don't you think? Anyway. He was mighty interested in this new brand of medication—S'Wellness, the stuff is called. Dumb name, if you ask me. It contains a rather deadly ingredient. It's is supposed to be making people better, but it has just enough of this ingredient to keep them sick. And even kill if they take too much of it. It has been recalled as of this morning."

Branson's eyes gleamed, his smile bright against his dark skin. Simon's smile, on the other hand, slipped further and further as Branson spoke.

"The CDC, FDA, and the New York Department of Health have all issued national safety alerts and the product is being pulled from all shelves. Won't take long because, for some reason Harmony is the only town that carries it. Isn't that odd?"

Branson took a step closer to Simon, and lifted his hands up, not as a gesture of surrender, but as a posture for prayer.

"Dear Lord," he said in a loud voice, "we rebuke Satan this day in Your name. We demand that Ol' Scratch remove himself from this town. He is no longer welcome here."

And then Simon's face twisted. Twisted into something not quite human.

"You still lost," Simon growled in a voice that was no longer his own.

James stepped up, side by side with Branson, and raised his hands in the same posture. "Lord, Jesus we know that your path is righteous, and on that path we walk. In Your name we rebuke Satan. He is no longer welcome in Harmony."

Simon gritted his teeth and clenched the brim of his hat.

"You won't kill any more," James said, more directly. "In the name of Jesus Christ we rebuke you Satan."

Simon's face slipped back to its human shape.

"You two think you're so smart," Simon screamed at them. "You think you've beaten me? Ha! You can't beat me! You can't stop me! You of all people should know that." Simon grabbed hold of the side mirror of the SUV he's been leaning on and gripped it harder and harder as he ranted, twisting it as though it were made of putty. It dropped to the ground and he stalked away into the early afternoon light.

James looked down at the mirror and saw the handprint burned into the plastic. "I hope they have insurance for that."

"You okay?" Branson asked.

James nodded. "I am." But he couldn't help feel that in this war, the devil might still be somehow winning.

CHAPTER
FORTY - FOUR

James swallowed a lump in his throat as he replayed their conversation with Simon over in his head. "You really have a friend at the CDC? I hope that wasn't a bluff."

"Not a bluff. My good friend, George Lehman is an epidemiologist. He works in New York, for a special branch of the CDC called the Epidemic Intelligence Service: E-I-S. You know how those government folk love their acronyms. Anyway, George is the go-to guy whenever there is an odd disease outbreak. He's a first responder."

"And you just happen to know this guy?" James couldn't believe their luck. "I thought you were bluffing for sure."

"Nope. We served in the Gulf War together."

"So what exactly did your friend discover?"

"Like I was telling our friend…this S'Wellness brand medicine is making people sick. You were right. It's not even real medicine."

James looked at him, incredulous. "How is it being sold then?"

"It's being marketed as a homeopathic vaccine."

"Like a flu vaccine?"

"Similar but not as safe and definitely not as regulated. George said these homeopathic preparations are made from bodily tissues and fluids taken from patients suffering from a disease. That sample is then sterilized and serially diluted, often to the point where no active ingredient remains. The problem is this particular concoction still contains a minute amount of the H1N1 virus."

"H1N1 virus?"

"The swine flu," Branson explained. "The same strain that killed an estimated fifty-million people worldwide during 1918 flu pandemic."

"And this H1N1 virus is in the S'Wellness medicine?"

"Yep."

"You think Simon—?"

Branson nodded. "Probably so. Satan or not, he is evil. It's a serious strain of the flu. And knowingly distributing it would make it domestic terrorism."

James tried to absorb all of this new information.

"Problem is they still don't have a way to connect

Simon to this mess," Branson continued. "And no one knows how this S'Wellness company got a hold of the virus or how it got into the medicine. It could have even been added by accident, which is why they need to locate the manufacturing plant."

"So there are people doing that now, right?"

"George was on the phone with Washington when I left him at my church. They issued a national bulletin, but no one seems to know where the plant is. There's no record of this S'Wellness company ever existing. It might not be a big factory, you know. It could even be someone's garage or basement."

"What about a local pharmacy?" James asked.

Branson narrowed his eyes. "That would make sense. They would have most of the equipment right there. What are you thinking?"

James could no longer stand still. He began to pace. "I bought that bottle of S'Wellness for Amy at Philip Falcone's pharmacy... Philip's wife died last night of the flu. And I found a bottle of it in the hospital room with John Colmenro's wife. I asked John where he got it and he said Philip gave it to him."

"Philip, huh? He strikes you as the type to instigate chemical warfare?"

"No, but lots of people are doing things they wouldn't normally do lately. Myself included." James shuddered at the memory of waking up in the hospital with his mind a total blank. "Simon could have dosed him with scopolamine, like he did to me."

"George said the medicine was distributed in a very localized area."

"You don't get more local than the center of town," James said.

The two men locked eyes before wordlessly getting into James' car. They had to get to the pharmacy. Philip could be in danger, or he could even be a real enemy. He might be preparing to release more of the virus. They had to move quickly.

"I'm calling George. I'll have him meet us at Falcone's." Branson said.

"With the power of God and the power of the law we are going to beat this!" James added.

CHAPTER FORTY-FIVE

James parked his Jetta in the nearly empty lot of Falcone's pharmacy under a glowing neon *closed* sign. The only other car was Phillip's.

"Where is your friend?" James asked.

"George will be here. It takes a few minutes to organize the cavalry…"

"We've got to get in there now, Branson."

"Hold on son, we don't know what we're dealing with in there. We need to wait for George and his team."

"The more people the more complicated it becomes. I don't want anyone to get hurt. I'm not waiting," James said, getting out the car. "I know Philip and if he is in there, I can talk to him."

Branson got out with him. He didn't bother to argue—he just peered into the windows of the darkened pharmacy and tried the door. It was locked. "Well, we're not going in the front door. Is there another way into this place?"

"I've seen trucks come to the back. There must be a delivery entrance there," James suggested.

"Okay, we'll check it out. But, I want you to stay behind me," Branson said. "I've had a little more experience with this sort of thing."

James followed his friend around the corner of the quiet building and into a narrow drive that butted up against the back of the building. There was a loading dock and a small brown door.

Branson turned to James with his finger in front of his lips, as they crept stealthily toward the door. James was happy to let Branson, an ex-serviceman, lead the way. His friend's sturdy exterior and calm manner made him feel safe, especially sneaking around a building.

Branson tried the knob. It turned easily, so he eased the door open. Thankfully, the door was well-oiled and didn't squeak. James followed him into a short, white-tiled hallway. Branson's feet made no sound even though he was wearing heavy boots.

The hallway ended abruptly and opened into a small workspace lit by a solitary lamp. Philip Falcone sat on the floor rocking back and forth, holding a bottle of S'Wellness and crying.

James stepped forward.

"Philip?" He called gently to the distraught

pharmacist.

Philip looked up and saw James. "Please tell me God will forgive me," he sobbed. "I thought it would help her. I thought I could help everyone. I got everything right. Why didn't it work?"

James knelt in front of him and tried to look him in the eyes, but Philip looked as if he hadn't stopped crying from the night before. His eyes rolled in his head and then he squeezed them shut.

"Philip, I'm sorry about Melissa," James said, in what he hoped was a soothing voice. "But I need you to tell me what's going on here. Where did you get this medicine?"

"It's not medicine, it's not," he choked and coughed the words. "It was supposed to be, it was supposed to help her. But it didn't. It didn't help her." He opened his eyes—a blood vessel had popped in one of them, giving it a dark red hue. "I failed her. Tell me I'll be forgiven."

James grabbed his shoulders and shook him gently. "Philip, I need you to focus! Where did the medicine come from? I need to know right now."

Philip blinked up at him like a stunned owl. "I formulated it here," he waved his arm toward his workstation, complete with a mortar and pestle and some glassware suspended over burners. It reminded James of his high school chemistry class.

Branson turned on his heel and went into the narrow hallway. James could hear him speaking into his cell phone updating George.

"Philip where did you get the virus?"

Philip stopped sobbing and looked up at James confused. "Virus? What virus?"

"The CDC analyzed your medicine and found it contains the H1N1 virus."

Philip looked genuinely confused. "H1N1? I don't understand. How could it?"

"It is making people sick, Philip. Where did you get the ingredients?"

Philip held his head in his hands and started sobbing again. "I formulated the medicine myself. Everything is off the shelf or over-the-counter. How could it be bad for people?"

"George has a Hazardous Materials crew on the way to shut this place down," Branson said, reentering the room. "He's still ten minutes out and wants us to stay put until his team gets here. I suppose it's a good thing we found this manufacturing facility so quickly."

"Manufacturing facility?" Philip asked. "This isn't the manufacturing facility."

James was confused. "Philip, you said you made the medicine yourself."

"I formulated it here. It's manufactured at the plant."

Branson lost his patience and his military persona took over. He crouched in front of Philip and grabbed him by the lapels of his lab coat and half-lifted him from the ground. "Who hired you? What are they planning?"

"I-I never met them, it was just some investors. They

hired me to create the formula and develop an aerosol delivery system. They said it was going to revolutionize the health industry."

"Aerosol version?" Branson's voice turned deadly cold. He shook Philip again, "I need you to straighten up and tell me what I need to know. Where is it being manufactured?"

"At the old meat packing plant, out on State Route 345, about fifteen minutes outside of town." He turned his bloodshot eyes to James. "I would never hurt anyone. I just wanted to help! You believe me, right?"

Branson shook the man again, more violently this time. "What are they planning?"

"They were supposed to ship out the aerosol tonight. But I told them it didn't work. They didn't listen. Said they made changes and only need my delivery system. Oh God, what have I done?"

James' heart skipped a beat. Simon must have added the H1N1 virus and now he had an airborne delivery system.

"What time? What time do the shipments go out?" Branson asked, setting Philip back on the ground.

"Five o'clock. At five o'clock trucks with the latest batch of S'Wellness are going out. The aerosol version, I mean."

James looked at the clock on the wall. They had less than twenty minutes. Simon had asked him to leave town several times and James had refused. So this was what Simon had been planning. He had to be stopped. If that virus gets airborne…

Every time they were close to figuring this out, it got stranger and more dangerous. There was so much on the line. How could he, a simple small town pastor, possibly fight a power like Simon's? Goodness would triumph over evil, but how was he going to stop this horrible thing from happening?

As if he knew what James was thinking, Branson held out a hand to James. "We are not alone."

James took his mentor's hand and was energized once again. He was still scared, but they had God's grace on their side.

The next instant, the small workspace came alive with a blinding light and a piercing sound that seemed to come from every direction at once.

James crouched, clapped his hands over his ears and squeezed his eyes shut against the disorienting chaos.

Before he had a chance to react, James was being thrown to the floor and his arms pulled roughly behind his back and fastened with some sort of zip-tie.

James opened his eyes. Everything was a blur. His ears were ringing and his other senses were dulled—was he dreaming?

What was happening?

CHAPTER FORTY-SIX

A dozen armed men wearing body armor and gas masks had entered Falcone's pharmacy. Several of them had weapons. Two of them picked up Philip who seemed to be unconscious. Two more were carrying Branson who looked James in the eye and mouthed something unintelligible to him as he passed by.

Branson was not resisting and James followed suit as he too was picked up and carried from the room. Other men wearing white coveralls complete with hoods were flowing in.

Outside, James was deposited face down on the grassy area next to the sidewalk beside Branson and Philip. A young man wearing a military uniform and a no-nonsense expression on his face stood over them with a deadly looking rifle.

James turned his head and could see that the parking lot was now full of military-looking vehicles and vans marked CDC and HAZ-MAT. Men in white coveralls were everywhere, even on the roof. James watched, fascinated as the little pharmacy was covered in plastic sheeting, like a home being fumigated for termites.

Gradually, his hearing began to return.

Men were barking orders, and powerful generators filled the air with a rough mechanical hum and a faint smell of diesel fuel.

"Where are they?" a voice said.

"This way, sir…" replied another.

Footsteps approached.

"Well, it's about time," said Branson.

"You've looked better," said the second, gruff voice.

"I've felt better too."

"Release them," said the gruff voice, and the young, no-nonsense guard bent down and cut the plastic restraints.

James rolled onto his back rubbing the soreness out of his wrists, not ready to attempt getting up just yet.

"What's wrong with that one?" said Gruff, motioning toward Philip.

"The stun grenade knocked him out, sir. He's been unconscious since we took them into custody, sir," answered No-Nonsense.

James turned his attention to Philip lying next to

him.

"Why isn't he getting medical attention?" barked Gruff.

"He's breathing, sir. Other than that… Things have been hectic sir."

"I want him more than breathing, soldier. I want him talking. This man may be the key to this whole operation."

The young soldier left in search of a medic.

"You Buchman?" Gruff asked, with an outstretched hand to James.

"I am." James took the man's hand and found it matched his appearance—cold, unyielding, and strong— definitely ex-military, and let himself be pulled to his feet.

"Name's George, George Lehman."

"Thanks for coming George," Branson said, and shook his hand as well. "I see you've brought friends."

Young soldier returned with a couple of paramedics who began examining Philip.

"This man is not to leave your sight, soldier," George told him. "Stay with him and have someone come get me the moment he can talk." He turned back to James and Branson. "I'd love to stand around and chit chat, gentlemen, but you see I have work to do here."

"Perhaps we can—" Branson began.

George cut him off. "Sorry, friend. This is far too dangerous for civilians."

"But this isn't the—"

"You and Buchman need to vacate the premises.

We'll handle it from here." With that, he turned on his heels and walked away.

James and Branson looked at each other.

"What about the plant?" James asked.

"I'll call him from the road," Branson said. "We haven't much time..."

CHAPTER
FORTY · SEVEN

James didn't know what they would do once they got to the old packing plant, but they had to do something. And it was likely that they were better equipped to battle Simon than the CDC was. This was going to be a case of spiritual warfare, not chemical warfare.

James buckled his seatbelt and gripped the steering wheel. He sped through town, but there wasn't a car in the world fast enough for him today. He slammed the accelerator to the floor.

They rode in silence, two men on a holy mission to protect those who could not protect themselves. James was willing to die to protect the town of Harmony, if need be. Branson pulled out a handkerchief and wiped the sweat from his brow. He was probably thinking the same thing.

The woods grew thicker, and the houses were farther apart. They would be at the plant soon. James just hoped it would be soon enough.

As they pulled into the cracked and patched parking lot, James slammed on the brakes to avoid colliding with a semi truck. Emblazoned across the side of the trailer was a logo:

S'Wellness™ Get Well Soon!

"Stop!" James yelled, as he leapt from the car before it came to a complete stop. He ran toward the truck. "Stop!"

He could see the driver, an older man in a baseball cap. He tried to wave him down, but the man didn't appear to see him. The truck just kept going, and when Branson came huffing up to James' side, he picked up a rock and threw it at the truck. It connected with a solid *thunk* but the truck kept driving.

"We're too late," Branson said, with tears in his eyes. The ten stall shipping dock was empty. "Looks like that was the last truck."

A wave of rage built inside James, but he pushed it down. Now was not the time for emotions and hurt pride. Now was the time to trust his fate to God and do what he could to fight evil. He turned to look at the old abandoned plant, but what he saw didn't make any sense. Was it possible that he was hallucinating?

Branson saw the puzzled look on James' face and looked toward the factory.

"What on earth…?"

It was Samuel. He was staggering toward the service entrance of the building carrying two large plastic jugs of gasoline in an eerie replay of his attempt to burn down James's church just one day before.

"I thought he was in the hospital?" James asked.

"He was…" Branson said. "On police watch."

"Must not have been a very close watch."

"He's not planning to burn down this building too, is he?"

"Let's hope not." James tried to think fast. "Samuel!" he called out.

Samuel turned, saw the two men, and tried to move faster.

"Check the offices and make sure they're empty," James said. "I'll try and stop him."

Branson nodded. "Be careful my friend," he said and then jogged toward the main entrance of the building.

The windows at the entrance of the tall, dust-colored building were tinted dark, and the door was ajar. If anyone was still inside Branson would help them escape.

CHAPTER FORTY-EIGHT

James turned back toward the service entrance, just in time to see Samuel duck inside the building. "Samuel! Stop!"

Samuel ignored him and disappeared into the building.

James ran toward the service entrance and hesitated just outside the door. He had to be cautious—after all, Simon could be inside. This could all just be a trap.

He poked his head inside the door and called Samuel's name again. It was dark and he could hear a scuffling sound and the whir of machinery. Gray metal control boxes lined the walls and a myriad of pipes and electrical conduit led from them, going up into the ceiling and down into the floor. It looked like the environmental controls and emergency generator were housed here, as well as a panel with the word *Sprinkler Control Valve* stenciled above it.

He went deeper into the dark, narrow room and turned a corner. A puddle of water was spreading across the floor. He kept walking.

"Samuel? I know you're in here! I just want to help."

"You're too late," Samuel called from the end of a row of semi-opaque water tanks. That must be where the water had come from. Several of them were empty, but when James squinted at Samuel's dark shape, he saw that the ones closest to the old man were full. It was then that the sharp smell of gasoline hit him in the face.

"What are you doing here, Samuel?"

"He thinks I don't remember, but I do," he muttered. He seemed confused, but not in a trance like he had been before. He finished pouring the gasoline into the tank. He held the jug far away from his body and was careful not to splash himself. "I'm going to stop him this time. I won't let him hurt any more people."

"Slow down, Samuel. What's going on here?"

Samuel didn't answer and walked into the main building through a maintenance door. James followed. On the other side of the door was a concrete hallway with wooden shelves full of cleaning supplies. Samuel picked up an old green duffel bag from one of the shelves and turned to James. "You can't be here, Reverend. This isn't your fight."

"I'm not leaving you Samuel. Not until you tell me

what's going on. How do you know about this place?" James followed Samuel, unsure of how to proceed. They reached a staircase and Samuel started up.

"I work here. Just two days a week. Enough to keep me busy," Samuel said, his breathing becoming more labored with each step. "I was working the day he showed up here. He tried to trick me into forgetting, but I'm old. I have systems in place to help me remember things. Knew he looked familiar, but thought it was impossible. But then strange things started happening. He made me kill me best friend, Reverend. I know he did. He needs to be stopped."

They reached the door to the second floor. Samuel paused to catch his breath, with sweat pouring into his eyes and his face pale as a ghost. "It's a virus he's making. I heard him talking. I saw them working in the lab here. And I know what God wants me to do. It's a good feeling, knowing what my purpose is, and that I'm so close to fulfilling it." He nodded toward the stairs and started up the third flight.

"I don't understand Samuel, what is your purpose here? Are you going to burn the building down? Why would God want you to burn the building? What if there are innocent people trapped inside?" James was concerned about Samuel, but the old man seemed at peace with his mission, whatever it was.

"Made sure everyone is out. I'll show you where he keeps it, the virus. He's planning on letting it out into the air. Get everyone sick. It's been his plan all along." He paused and panted heavily, holding the rail. "They call it the clean room, though what it holds is foul." He started up the last few stairs to the third floor, moving slowly and painfully.

"Samuel, you're not looking too well—"

"I've never been better, Reverend," he said. And as they reached the third floor landing, he turned to James and smiled. "Almost…there."

Despite his obvious physical discomfort, there was a light shining in Samuel's eyes that James hadn't ever seen before.

What was God's plan was for the retired veteran?

CHAPTER
FORTY-NINE

James and Samuel entered the third floor into a bright white hallway lined on one side with glass windows. James saw a sign that read, *Clean Room, Authorized Personnel Only* above a thick-looking glass door.

"I know the code. I'm going to reverse the pump that's set to release the virus, and make it flow back into the clean room. Then I'll set off my surprise." He tapped the duffle bag he carried and chuckled. "But I got to do it fast, before he gets here." His eyes darkened. "Once inside, I've planned my escape, but you need to leave now... Make sure people stay away from this building. Keep them far, far, away, Reverend. Can you do that for me?"

Branson burst through the stairwell door and saw

James and Samuel.

"James!" He tried to catch his breath. "It's Simon, he's here!"

In the split second when James looked away from Samuel, the crafty older man tapped a code into the keypad and entered the clean room. When James turned back toward him, the door sucked shut behind him.

"Samuel, no! Don't do this!" He pulled at the handle, but it was futile. The door was built to keep certain things out and other things in.

Branson went into an office and dragged out a heavy wooden chair. He threw it against the door over and over, but the chair took more damage than the door.

James watched helplessly as Samuel calmly lit an unfiltered cigarette and balanced it on a stack of papers on a desk in the clean room. Then he took what looked like a pipe bomb out of his duffle bag and fiddled with it for a moment. He put it back in the bag and set it down on the ground and headed toward a control panel on the wall, stumbling and sweating.

"He's reversing the airflow to release the virus into the clean room. Then he's setting off a bomb," James told Branson.

"What was he doing with the gasoline?"

"He replaced the water in the fire sprinkler tanks."

Branson's eyes widened in panic, and he redoubled his efforts to open the door. "James, do you know what he's done?"

Samuel came to the door but didn't open it. "I've got to reverse the flow!" He shouted, but they could only faintly hear him. Get out now! I'll follow once I've got the settings right. Keep everyone away. You've got about five minutes to get out of here, I suggest you start running!"

Branson gripped his shoulder. "James, we've got to go, and we've got to go now!"

"We can't just leave him here."

"I've seen this before—in Kuwait. He's created a makeshift air-fuel explosive. When that bomb goes off, igniting the gasoline, it's going to create a massive fireball that will consume everything in its path. We need to go!"

James picked up the chair Branson had been using and started pounding on the door. "We've got to get him out of there."

"James, it is no use. You're not going to get in and he's not coming out. Not until he does what he feels he needs to do."

James watched helplessly as Samuel continued working at the control panel. He seemed to be getting weaker by the moment, but determined to finish what he had started. In the glass door, James could see his own reflection and that of his friend and mentor standing beside him. "We've come all this way, Branson. God led us here for a reason. I truly believe that. We can't leave him here alone."

"He's not alone. Maybe Samuel is right where God wants him to be. And maybe God brought us here to make sure Samuel got to where he needed to go."

James fought back the emotions that were coursing through his veins.

"Samuel, look at me!" James screamed through the thick glass.

The frail man stopped moving for a moment, went to the door, and stared directly into James' eyes.

"God is with you," James mouthed to the piercing blue eyes that were just inches away. He wanted to say more—a prayer or other powerful words to give Samuel strength—

"We've got to get out of here now, in case this hair-brained scheme doesn't work!" Branson said, grabbing James by the arm and dragging him a few feet down the hallway.

Half way to the staircase, both men started running, followed by a panicked descent down to the exit.

CHAPTER FIFTY

—

The old one was fumbling with the control panel. What did he think he was going to do?

"Samuel, I see you," Simon taunted.

The old man was startled, and that pleased him.

"Get behind me, Satan!" Samuel cried out. His stiff, arthritic fingers tried to turn a wheel that would reverse the flow of air in the clean room, flooding it with the virus in aerosol form.

"I won't get sick, Samuel. All this is for nothing. I saw your friends running away, the priests. They can't help you now. I'm going to win, and you will have helped me ever so much. In fact, I couldn't have done it without you." His sinister laugh echoed pleasingly in the sealed room.

"Lord help me, give me strength."

"Do you really think your God is going to help you now?"

"I know He will. This is His plan. I am merely His instrument."

Samuel's hands were weak, but he finally managed to turn the wheel that reversed the flow. A rush of super-cooled air began filling the room. The effort left him exhausted and he fell to the floor. His suffering made Simon laugh all the more as he approached the old man lying on the ground.

The old man tried to get up and make his way to the exit, but Simon pushed him back down.

"You're old, and you're weak. You can't defeat me, you must know that!"

He allowed Samuel to rise and stumble a few feet toward the door before he took two effortless steps and stood squarely in front of it to block his path. "You're not leaving!"

Samuel sank to his knees and clutched his chest.

"You're not looking so good old man. I'm going to enjoy watching you sicken yourself with my plague. I've never seen what such a large dose will do to someone, so thanks for that."

Samuel fought to stand again, but suddenly the blood drained from his face and his head began to shake just the tiniest bit. Simon watched as the old man had a heart attack. Samuel's eyes rolled back into their sockets and he fought to keep his eyelids open.

And suddenly, he was limp on the floor in front of Simon.

Simon kicked the body halfheartedly. He knelt and took the old man's withered wrist in his hand to check for a pulse. It was cold and clammy, but he was still alive.

Barely.

"You're not as young as you used to be, Samuel."

A wisp of smoke rose from a stack of papers.

As he turned to investigate, the sprinklers came on and the room filled with the smell of gasoline. The smoke stopped, and Simon saw the tiny glow disappear as the cigarette that had been left to burn winked out.

Simon threw his head back and laughed. His mouth filled with gasoline, but he didn't care. It tasted like death, and death was his constant companion.

He laughed at the futility of Samuel's final attempt to stop him. He had to admit, he hadn't expected the old man to fill the water tanks with gasoline. That was clever. But the pipes still had a bit of water in them and that had been enough to extinguish the cigarette before it had the chance to ignite the gasoline.

"You stupid old man. You thought you could beat me with a cigarette? A CIGARETTE?" He screamed down at Samuel, who lay prone on the floor, unmoving.

Simon danced across the room, stomping and splashing in the growing puddles of gasoline. His toe touched something hard. It was a small green duffel bag. He gave it a kick and something skittered out onto the floor. Simon looked closer.

A tiny digital clock, attached to a metal pipe, flashed red numbers at him.

00:04...

00:03...

00:02...

"Noooo!" Simon howled.

His cry was cut off by the massive explosion that sucked all the air from the room and blasted out all of the windows in the same millisecond.

*   *   *

JAMES AND BRANSON WERE nearly two miles away but the force from the explosion was still enough to shatter the back and side windows of the Jetta.

The explosion annihilated everything within five hundred yards of the site. Up to five miles away windows blew out of buildings. The ground shook in Oak Falls, about forty miles away and the sound of the explosion was heard in the next state.

James and Branson were shook up, but uninjured.

"Do you think he made it out?" James asked hopefully as he shook cubes of glass from his hair.

"I don't think so, son. He may have tried, but I don't think he had enough time. And I doubt anything could have survived that explosion, including the virus."

James said a silent prayer with a mixture of gratefulness and sadness in his heart.

CHAPTER FIFTY-ONE

They had stood up to the devil, and the devil lost. So why didn't James feel good about it?

Well, possibly because sixteen people died—died before he and his parishioners had gone door-to-door and offered to pray with those who were sick—died before he and Branson were able to get the medication recalled and the delivery trucks stopped.

They had done their best and sixteen people were dead.

James sat in a corner booth at Ed's Diner and took another sip of his coffee. Tomorrow was another day, as they say, and God help him if he wouldn't be doing his best then too.

An unusually early snow had started to fall. The world didn't stop just because bad things happened to good people.

Amy joined him and while they waited for their breakfast, he told her everything.

Everything.

About Daniel and Rick and the scopolamine…

About St. Joseph, the town in Florida…

About Charles Griffin, the former pastor of New Hope Church…

About S'Wellnes and the H1N1 virus…

He held nothing back.

He explained that he believed Satan had taken the form of a man, calling himself Simon Paradis, and had walked around Harmony, causing all this mayhem.

And then he explained how George, Branson's friend from the CDC, said Samuel's last minute heroics helped save millions of lives… but at the cost of his own.

When he was finished he waited for her to laugh at him, or look at him like he was crazy, to tell him she couldn't possibly be with a religious nut like him.

Instead, she reached over and took his hand. "I believe you," she said. "And, I'm proud of you."

James sighed out the breath he'd been holding. He should never have hidden this truth from Amy. Not from her. He should have trusted her to believe him.

She had become more than just his friend.

She was his strength.

"What if he's still alive? What will you do if he comes back?" Amy asked.

He leaned in closer to her across the table and took her hand in his. "I will depend on my best friend to know which wire to pull and believe that God will send her to me in time to pull it."

Her eyes misted over as he said it. "I plan to be right here with you, James."

James was happier this morning than he had been in a very long time. He looked forward to spending his life in Harmony, ministering to its people.

And loving the woman sitting across from him.

EPILOGUE

Six months later

The phone rang in the middle of the night. At least, he thought it was the middle of the night. He was too tired to read the red numbers on his digital alarm clock. It was late. That was all he knew.

Being a pastor in a small town like Harmony meant your phone could ring at all hours of the night.

Cecilia Miller mumbled, "Hello?" but wasn't quite awake enough to pick up the receiver.

"I've got it, baby." Reverend Branson Miller reached over her and picked up the handset. He thumbed the green button to connect the call. "Hello?"

"Uncle Branson?" The voice was whisper soft and familiar.

"Claire? Claire, what're you doing calling this late? Is everything okay? Do you know what time it is?"

There was a pause on the line. "It's only ten o'clock here."

"Yeah, but you're out there in California and I'm here in my nice warm bed in New York." He laughed, coming fully awake.

"Is it Claire?" Cecilia asked sleepily.

"Yes, it's Claire, go back to sleep." Branson took the phone into the living room and sat in his favorite recliner. "It's so good to hear from you! What's it been, two years?"

"Three, almost three. I'm so sorry to bother you."

"No bother. Not for my most favorite niece. What's up?"

Another pause, longer this time.

He could hear her breathing hard. "Uncle, I don't know what to do. He's here. He's...he's going to do something bad, I just know it."

Now Branson stood up out and turned on the light. "Who's there, honey? What's going on?"

He hadn't seen Claire, his baby sister's kid, in so long. Now to hear from her like this was almost too much. They had always been close when she was younger. The thought of anyone hurting her was unbearable.

"He's...he's calling himself Simon. But it's him, I know it is."

Branson's blood ran cold. The light he had just turned on didn't seem bright enough.

"Hold on, honey. Start from the beginning."

But before Claire could explain the phone went dead.

Branson called back.

Straight to voicemail.

He tried again.

Straight to voicemail again. "Claire? Claire, are you there? It's Uncle Branson, call me back. I'm worried!"

He punched in another number—the one person on earth that could help. The phone rang only a few times before James Buchman answered.

"Morning, James. Pack your bags. We're going to California."

ABOUT THE AUTHOR

Daniel Patterson is the author of the #1 bestselling religious fiction mystery, *One Chance*. Before turning his attention to writing, Daniel spent his days working as an executive in the Internet industry. A San Francisco native, Daniel currently resides in Southern California where he is busy working on the second book in *The Devil's Game* series.

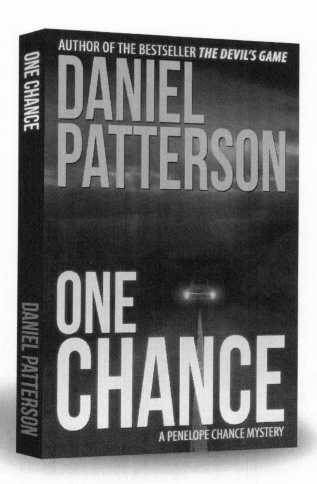

AUTHOR OF THE BESTSELLER *THE DEVIL'S GAME*

DANIEL PATTERSON

ONE CHANCE

DANIEL PATTERSON

ONE CHANCE

A PENELOPE CHANCE MYSTERY

What would you do if your best friend was accused of murder?

ONE CHANCE

With the exception of a double homicide twenty-three years ago, nothing significant ever happens in the tiny town of Franklin, Florida. In spite of her prayers, the truth was sometimes Officer Penelope Chance wished a big case would cross her desk. Something to get her blood pumping.

So when she gets a call about an attempted murder, she can't help but get excited. But when she learns who the victim is...and who is suspected of the crime... her blood runs cold. What starts out as an attempted murder quickly turns into a murder mystery that's going to leave Penelope questioning her faith in the people around her and herself.

Available now, *One Chance* the first book in the Penelope Chance Mystery Series.